Lily gasped. "Is this a joke?"

She stared at her reflection—their reflection—in the mirror. At the darkness of his fingers against her skin, her hair wild and tumbling around her shoulders in a silky mess. Her pink cotton shirt was stained over the left shoulder, and her eyes, though tired, gleamed with fury. Nico, in contrast, was cool and unruffled. If not for his quickened heartbeat against her, she'd almost think him bored.

But, no, there it was—that flash of something in his eyes, in the set of his jaw, that spoke volumes without a sound being uttered.

"No joke, Liliana. I have broken a long-sought-after treaty between my country and Monteverde, not to mention embarrassed my father and our allies, so that I can do what should have been done the instant you conceived my child."

"I—I don't understand," she whispered, searching his face in the mirror, her heart slamming into her ribs.

"Of course you do," he replied, dipping his head until his lips almost grazed the shell of her ear. Almost, but not quite. "You, Miss Lily Morgan, are about to become the crown princess—my consort and the mother of my children."

Happy New Year!

This is certainly the year for Harlequin Presents® fans; we have so much to offer you in 2010 that the New Year cheer will just keep on sparkling!

As if the Presents line wasn't already jam-packed full of goodies, we're bringing you more with three fabulous new miniseries! The glamour, the excitement, the intensity just keep getting better.

In January look out for *Powerful Italian, Penniless Housekeeper* by India Grey, the first book in AT HIS SERVICE, the miniseries that features your favourite humble housekeepers swept off their feet by their gorgeous bosses! He'll show her that a woman's work has never been so much fun!

We all love a ruthless marriage bargain, and that's why we're bringing you BRIDE ON APPROVAL. Whether bought, sold, bargained for or bartered, these brides have no choice but to say I do. Be sure not to miss Caitlin Crews's debut book, *Pure Princess, Bartered Bride* in February.

Last but by no means least, we're presenting some devilishly handsome, fiercely driven men who have dragged themselves up from nothing to become some of the richest men in the world. These SELF-MADE MILLIONAIRES are so irresistible they have a miniseries all their own!

January and February see the final two installments of the wonderful ROYAL HOUSE OF KAREDES. But the saga continues in a different setting from April as we introduce four gorgeous, brooding sheikhs with a hint of Karedes about them, in DARK-HEARTED DESERT MEN! Four desert princes, four brilliant stories.

Wow! 2010—this truly is the year of Presents!
Your everyday luxury.

Lynn Raye Harris

CAVELLI'S LOST HEIR

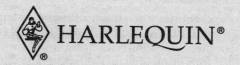

HARLEQUIN®

TORONTO • NEW YORK • LONDON
AMSTERDAM • PARIS • SYDNEY • HAMBURG
STOCKHOLM • ATHENS • TOKYO • MILAN • MADRID
PRAGUE • WARSAW • BUDAPEST • AUCKLAND

Recycling programs
for this product may
not exist in your area.

ISBN-13: 978-0-373-12887-7

CAVELLI'S LOST HEIR

First North American Publication 2010.

Copyright © 2009 by Lynn Raye Harris.

All about the author...
Lynn Raye Harris

LYNN RAYE HARRIS read her first Harlequin romance when her grandmother carted home a box from a yard sale. She didn't know she wanted to be a writer then, but she definitely knew she wanted to marry a sheikh or a prince and live the glamorous life she read about in the pages. Instead, she married a military man and moved around the world. She's been inside the Kremlin, hiked up a Korean mountain, floated on a gondola in Venice and stood inside volcanoes at opposite ends of the world.

These days Lynn lives in North Alabama with her handsome husband and two crazy cats. When she's not writing, she loves to read, shop for antiques, cook gourmet meals and try new wines. She is also an avowed shoeaholic and thinks there's nothing better than a new pair of high heels.

Lynn was a finalist in the 2008 Romance Writers of America Golden Heart® contest, and she is the winner of the Harlequin Presents Instant Seduction contest. She loves a hot hero, a heroine with attitude and a happy ending. Writing passionate stories for Harlequin is a dream come true. You can visit Lynn at www.lynnrayeharris.com.

To Mom and Pop, who took me to live in fascinating places, bought me lots of books, and didn't blink when I locked myself in my room for hours on end to read.

CHAPTER ONE

CROWN PRINCE NICO CAVELLI, of the Kingdom of Montebianco, sat at a fourteenth-century antique desk and reviewed a stack of paperwork his assistant had brought him an hour ago. A glance at his watch told him there were several hours yet before he had to dress and attend the State dinner given in honor of his engagement to a neighboring princess.

Nico had a sudden urge to loosen his collar—except it was already loose. Why did the thought of marriage to Princess Antonella make him feel as if a noose were tightening around his neck?

So much had changed in his life recently. A little over two months ago he was the younger son, the dissolute playboy prince. The prince with a new mistress every few weeks, and with nothing more pressing to do than to decide which party to attend each night. It wasn't the whole truth of his existence, though it was the one the media enjoyed writing stories about. He'd been content to let them, to feed their need for scandalous behavior. Anything to keep their attention away from his emotionally fragile brother.

Nico pinched the bridge of his nose.

Gaetano had been the oldest. The delicate one. The legitimate one.

The brother that Nico had spent his childhood protecting

when he hadn't been fighting for his own honor as the product of a royal indiscretion. Ultimately, he couldn't protect Gaetano from the ramifications of his choices, or from the fateful decision to aim his Ferarri at a cliff and jam the pedal to the floor.

Per Dio, he missed Gaetano so much. And he was angry with him. Angry that he'd chosen such finality, that he hadn't fought harder against his personal demons, that he hadn't trusted Nico with his secret years ago. Nico would have moved mountains for Gaetano if he'd known.

"Basta!" Nico muttered, focusing again on the paperwork. Nothing would bring Gaetano back, and nothing would change Nico's destiny now. He was the remaining prince, and though he was illegitimate, the Montebiancan constitution allowed him to inherit. In this day and age, with modern medicine being what it was, there was no doubt of his parentage—if, indeed, there could be any doubt in the first place; Cavelli men always looked as if they'd been cast from the same mold.

Only Queen Tiziana disapproved of Nico's new status—but then she'd disapproved of him his whole life. Nothing he ever did had been good enough for her. He'd tried to please her when he'd been a child, but he'd always been shut out. He understood now, as a grown man, why she'd disliked him. His presence reminded her that her husband had been unfaithful.

When he'd moved into the palace after his mother's death, the queen had seen him as a threat, especially because he was stronger and bigger than Gaetano, though he was the younger of the two. That he was now Crown Prince only drove the pain deeper. He was a constant reminder of what she'd lost. It didn't matter that he'd also loved Gaetano, that he would give anything for his brother to still be alive.

Since he couldn't bring Gaetano back, he would do his utmost to fulfill his duty as Crown Prince to the best of his ability. It was the only way to honor his brother's memory.

A knock on the door brought his head up. "Enter."

"The Prefect of Police has sent a messenger, Your Highness," his assistant said.

"I will see him," Nico replied.

A moment later, a uniformed man appeared and bowed deeply. "Your Serene Highness, the Prefect sends his greetings."

Nico tamped down his impatience as the man recited the ritual greetings and wishes for his health and happiness. "What is the message?" he asked, somewhat irritably, once the formalities had been observed.

Though it was indeed the Crown Prince's duty to oversee the police force, it was more a symbolic role than anything else. That the Prefect was actually communicating with him about something filled him with an uncharacteristic sense of foreboding.

Ridiculous. It was merely the awareness of his loss of freedom that pinched at the back of his mind and made him feel uneasy.

The man reached into his inner pocket and pulled out an envelope. "The Prefect has tasked me with informing you that we have recovered some of the ancient statues taken from the museum. And to give you this, Your Highness."

Nico held out his hand. The man stood to attention while Nico ripped into the envelope.

He expected the sheet of paper inside, but it was the photograph of a woman and child that caught Nico's attention first. Their faces filled the frame as if someone had stood very close to snap the picture. He recognized the woman almost instantly—the wheat-blond hair, the green eyes and the smattering of freckles across her nose—and felt a momentary pang of regret their liaison had not lasted longer. His gaze skimmed to the child.

Sudden fury corroded his insides. *It was not possible.* He

had never been that careless. He would never do to a child what had been done to him. He would never father a baby and walk away. It had to be a trick, a stunt to embarrass him on the eve of his engagement, a ploy to get money. There was no way this child was his.

His mind reeled. He'd spent only a short time with her, had made love to her only once—much to his regret. Wouldn't he have remembered if something had gone wrong? Of course he would—but the child had the distinct look of a Cavelli. Nico couldn't tear his gaze away from eyes that were a mirror to his own as he unfolded the paper. Finally, he succeeded in wrenching his attention to the Prefect's scrawled words.

Nico dropped the paper and shoved back from the desk. "You will take me to the prison. Now."

Lily Morgan was desperate. She was only supposed to be in Montebianco for two days. She'd been here for three. Her heart beat so loud and hard in her ears that she'd half expected to have a heart attack hours ago. She had to get home, had to get back to her baby. But the authorities showed no signs of letting her leave, and her pleas to speak with the American Consulate were ignored. She hadn't seen a soul in over four hours now. She knew because she still had her watch, though they'd taken her cell phone and laptop away when they'd brought her down here.

"Hey!" she yelled. *"Hey! Is anyone there?"*

No one answered. There was nothing but the echo of her voice against the ancient stone interior of the old fortress.

Lily sank onto the lumpy mattress in the dank cell and scraped her hand beneath her nose. She would not cry. Not again. She had to be strong for her boy. Would he miss her by now? She'd never left him before. She would not have done so now had her boss not given her little choice.

"Julie's sick," he'd said about the paper's only travel writer just a few days ago. "We need you to go to Montebianco and research that piece she was working on for the anniversary edition."

Lily had blinked, dumbfounded. "But I've never written a travel article!" In fact, she'd never written anything more exciting than an obituary in the three months she'd been at the paper. She wasn't even a journalist, though she'd hoped to become one someday. She'd been hired to work in the advertising department, but since the paper was small, she often did double duty when there was a shortage.

The only reason the *Port Pierre Register* had a travel writer was because Julie was not only the publisher's niece, but her parents also owned the town's single travel agency. If she was writing about Montebianco, there was probably a special package deal coming up.

But the mere thought of traveling to Montebianco had turned Lily's legs to jelly. How could she enter the Mediterranean kingdom knowing that Nico Cavelli lived there?

Her boss was oblivious. "You don't need to write it, sweetheart. Julie's done most of the work already. Just go take some pictures, write down how it feels to be there, that kind of thing. Experience the country for two days, then come back and work with her on the write-up."

When she demurred, he refused to take no for an answer. "Times are getting tough, Lily. If I can't count on you to do the job when I need you, I may have to find someone who's more willing. This is your chance to prove yourself."

Lily couldn't afford to lose her position at the paper. Jobs weren't exactly thick on the ground in Port Pierre; without this one, she couldn't pay her rent or keep up with her medical insurance premiums. She could search for other employment, but there was no guarantee she'd find anything quickly. Once she'd gotten pregnant, she'd had to drop out of college. She'd spent the last couple of years bouncing from one low-paying position to another, doing anything to take care of her baby.

The job at the paper was a major break and a huge step up for her. She might even be able to return to school part-time and finish her studies someday.

She simply could not endanger Danny's future by refusing. She'd gone without many things as a child when her mother had been out of work or, worse, had dropped everything to run off with her womanizing father again. Lily would not do that to her own baby. She'd learned the hard way never to rely on anyone but herself.

She had no choice but to accept the assignment, though she'd comforted herself with the knowledge that her chances of actually crossing paths with a prince were pretty slim. She would leave Danny with her best friend, spend two days touring Castello del Bianco, and then she would be on a plane home. Simple, right?

But she'd never bargained on winding up in a prison cell. Would someone call the authorities when she didn't return? Had they already done so? It was her only hope—that someone would report her missing and the American Consulate would insist upon an accounting of her movements within the kingdom.

A distant clanging brought Lily to her feet. Her heart thumped harder if it were possible. Was someone coming to see her, to let her go? Or was it simply a new prisoner being brought into the depths of this musty old fortress?

Lily gripped the bars and peered down the darkened hall. Footsteps echoed in the ancient corridor. A voice spoke until another silenced it with a sharp command. She swallowed, waiting. A lifetime later, a man came into view, his form too dark beneath the shadows to distinguish features. He stopped just short of the pale light knifing down from a slit in the fortress wall several feet above his head. He didn't speak.

Lily's heart dropped to her toes as a fresh wave of tears

threatened. Oh God, he couldn't be here. *He simply couldn't.* Fate could not be so cruel.

She couldn't say a word as the prince—for so she had to think of him—moved into the light. And—oh my—he was every bit as handsome as the pictures in the magazines made him out to be. As her memory insisted he was. His black hair was shorter than she remembered, as if he'd cropped it closer in an effort to look more serious. He wore dark trousers and a casual silk shirt unbuttoned over a fitted T-shirt. Ice-blue eyes stared back at her from a face so fine it appeared as if an artist had molded it.

My God, had she really thought he was just a graduate student at Tulane when she'd met him at Mardi Gras? Could she have been any more naive? There was no way this man could ever be mistaken for anything other than what he was: a wealthy, privileged person who moved in circles so far above her that she got altitude sickness just thinking about it.

"Leave us," he said to the man at his side.

"But Your Highness, I do not think—"

"Vattene via!"

"Si, Mio Principe," the man answered in the Italian dialect commonly spoken in Montebianco. He gave a short bow and scurried up the passageway. Lily held her breath.

"You are accused of trying to smuggle Montebiancan antiquities out of the country," he said coolly, once the echoes from the man's footsteps faded away.

Lily blinked. "I'm sorry?" Of all the things she'd expected him to say, this had not been even a remote possibility.

"Two figurines, *signorina.* A wolf and a lady. They were found in your luggage."

"Souvenirs," she sputtered in disbelief. "I bought them from a street vendor."

"They are priceless treasures of my country's heritage, stolen from the state museum three months ago."

Lily's knees went weak. *Oh, God.* "I know nothing about that! I just want to go home."

Her pulse hammered in her ears. It was all so strange. Both the accusation and the fact he didn't appear to recognize her. But of course he wouldn't! Had she really expected it? She gave her head a tiny shake. No, she hadn't, but after all she'd been through the last two years, it hurt nonetheless. How could he not look at her and know? How could he not be aware of her the way she was of him?

Prince Nico drew closer. His hands were thrust in his pockets as he gazed down at her, his cool eyes giving nothing away. No hint of recognition, no sliver of kindness, nothing. Just supreme arrogance and a sense of entitlement so complete it astonished her. Had she really spent hours talking with this man? About *what?*

Without meaning to, she remembered lying beneath him, feeling his body moving inside hers. It had all been so new to her, and yet he'd been tender and reassuring. He'd made her feel special, cherished.

Now, the memory seemed like a distant illusion, made all the more so by his lack of awareness of it.

She dropped her gaze, unable to maintain the contact. His eyes were unusual in their coloring, pale and striking, but that wasn't the precise reason she couldn't look at him.

No, she couldn't look because it made her heartsick for her child. She hadn't realized it until she was face-to-face with the prince again, but Danny was the exact image of his father.

"I am afraid that is impossible."

Her head snapped up, her eyes beginning to tear again. *No.* She had to be strong. "I—I have to get home. I have responsibilities. People need me."

Prince Nico's gaze sharpened. "What people, *signorina?*"

Lily's stomach hollowed with fear. She couldn't tell him about Danny, not now. Not like this. "My family needs me. My mother depends on me." She hadn't seen her mother in over a year, but he didn't know that.

He studied her, his quick gaze sweeping over her with interest. And something more. Her nerve endings prickled.

"No husband, Lily?"

His use of her name was like the subtle caress of his fingers against her skin: shocking, unexpected and delicious. At first she thought he must recognize her, must remember her name after all—though he'd called her *Liliana* in their time together. But nothing in his demeanor indicated he had. *He'd gotten it from the police. Of course.*

She felt like a fool for thinking otherwise. But why was he here? Did a prince really come to the prison when someone was accused of theft? She felt as though she was missing a piece of the puzzle, as though there was something she should know, but she couldn't quite grasp what it was.

"No, no husband," she said. She couldn't mention Danny, she simply couldn't. Fear for her baby threatened to overwhelm her. If Nico knew he had a son, would he take her baby away from her? He certainly had the power and the money to do so.

She pressed closer to the bars, beseeching him, pouring every ounce of feeling she had into her words. "*Please,* Ni— Your Highness," she corrected, thinking better of calling him by name. "*Please* help me."

She thought he looked puzzled, but it was gone so fast she couldn't be sure.

"How is it you expect me to help you?"

Lily swallowed the hard knot in her throat. Could she confess just a little bit? Would she endanger her baby by doing so? Or was she endangering him by not speaking? What if she never got out of here? Would Carla raise Danny as her own? "W-we met once. In New Orleans two years ago. You were kind to me then."

If she expected awareness to cross his features, she was disappointed. He remained distant, detached.

"I am always kind to women." His voice was as smooth and rich as chocolate. And as cool as an Alpine lake.

Heat rushed to Lily's face. How could she stand here and have this conversation with him, with the man who'd fathered her child and didn't even know it? She'd been right about him, right not to persist in her efforts to track him down once she'd learned he was so much more than an ordinary man named Nico Cavelli.

She still remembered the shock of finding out who he really was, the endless parade of photos and sensational tabloid articles once she'd discovered his identity. Prince Nico of Montebianco was nothing more than a playboy, a jet-setter on a global scale who'd once gone slumming in New Orleans. He did not remember her, did not care about her, and certainly wouldn't care about Danny.

Just as her father hadn't cared about her or her mother. Of all the men in this world, how had she chosen *this* one to initiate her into the ways of intimacy between a man and a woman? It was mind-boggling how ignorant she'd been, how duped she'd been by his charm and sincerity. He hadn't exactly lied about who he was, but he hadn't told the truth, either. She'd known his name and where he was from, but she hadn't known he was a prince until later.

Once he'd gotten what he wanted from her, he'd abandoned her to her fate. She'd stood in the rain for over two hours that last night, waiting for him. He'd promised he would be there, but he never showed.

God, he made her sick.

Before she could gather her thoughts to speak, to think of another method of approach, he whipped something from his shirt pocket and thrust it toward her. Gone was the cool facade. In its place was a wrath so deep it would have frightened her had there been no bars between them.

"What is the meaning of this? Who is this child?"

Lily's heart squeezed. She shoved her hand between the bars, tried to reach the picture of her and Danny, but the prince snatched it away. A sob tore from her throat before she could stop it. They'd gone through her things, dismantled her suitcases as if she was a common thief and passed her possessions around for comment. Worst of all—*he knew her secret!*

"Who is he?" the prince demanded again.

"That's my baby! Give me that," she cried, clawing between the bars. "It's mine!"

He looked furious. And a little bit stunned, if that were possible. But he recovered quickly. "I don't know what you think will happen now that I've seen this, but it will not work, *signorina*. This is a cheap attempt to blackmail me, and I will not bow to it." His voice dripped menace.

Lily stopped struggling and stared at him, her head buzzing with emotion. "Blackmail you? Why would I do that? I want *nothing* from you!"

Her mind raced. Nico didn't know anything for certain. He was only concerned about himself and his money. If she hadn't been locked up, it might have been a relief in an odd way to have her opinion of him confirmed. She had to make sure he understood that she expected nothing from him. If he didn't feel threatened, he might help her to leave this place.

Lily closed her eyes, struggled for calm. "All I want is to go home."

Why had she ever been worried he would take her baby away? He was not the kind of man who would care about his child. He kept many mistresses, and had fathered several children already. She usually avoided the gossip magazines, but the occasional blaring headline about Nico still had the power to attract her attention. She knew, for instance, that he was about to marry.

A pang of feeling sliced into her and she pushed it down deep without examining it. How must his wife-to-be feel about his philandering ways, about the many children with no real father? She had certainly made the right decision not to get in touch with him two years ago. Danny deserved so much better than a father like him, a father who would never be bothered to spend any time getting to know his child. She didn't want her baby to grow up the way she did, with a wastrel father who only came into her life whenever it suited him—and left it again without concern for the emotional wreckage strewn in his wake.

"What are you doing in Montebianco?" he demanded, his tone distrustful and suspicious. "Why did you come here, if not to try and blackmail me?"

"I was doing research," she said, her temper flaring. "For a newspaper article. And why would I want to blackmail you?"

"Do not play games with me, *signorina.*" He tucked the photo back into his pocket. He looked murderous, as if he could order the guard to forget she was down here and throw away the key. A sliver of fear knifed into her; he probably *could* do such a thing.

"I hope you are comfortable, Lily Morgan, because you are going to spend as much time in this cell as it takes for me to learn the truth."

"I told you my boss sent me. I didn't come for any other reason!"

"You do not wish to tell me this child in the photo is mine? You did not come all this way to do just that? To demand money?"

Lily wrapped her arms around her body, surprised she was trembling, and looked away. "No. I want to go home and forget I ever met you."

Nico moved so fast she jerked back a step, forgetting the bars between them. His hands were the ones gripping the metal this time, his pale gaze lasering into her. "I don't know what you're playing at, Miss Morgan, but I assure you I will get to the truth."

When he shoved away and strode up the passage, she didn't make a sound. It wouldn't have mattered anyway. Prince Nico had no heart.

Nico strode into his apartments in the palace and summoned his assistant. Once he gave the order to find out everything about Miss Margaret Lily Morgan—oh yes, that had been a surprise, finding out she used her middle name instead of her first; and yet it explained why he'd never found a trace of her when he'd inquired two years ago—he went onto the terrace and gazed out at the city below.

The encounter had affected him more than he cared to admit. Lily Morgan was not at all what he expected. She was not the soft, almost shy girl he remembered, his Liliana who was as pure and fine as the flower she was named after. The night in prison should have frightened her, made her cooperative. Yet this Lily was fierce, determined.

But determined to do what?

He did not know, but he would not leave her there for another night—was, in fact, somewhat appalled she'd been held there without his knowledge in the first place. Nico's mouth twisted in distaste. It made sense that the old fortress was still used as a prison, but the conditions could be improved. Yet another thing he would change now that he was Crown Prince.

He slipped the photo from his pocket, held it between two fingers without looking at it. The photograph had been altered, he was sure of it. Any talented photographer with the right computer equipment could make a photo say anything he or she wanted it to say. How well Nico knew this. Today was not the first time he'd been presented with such a lie. The media tried all the time to place him somewhere he'd not been, or with someone he'd not been with. The photographs were doctored, easily disproved, though it was irritating and inconvenient to do so.

And yet it was the life he'd chosen, when he'd chosen to be the foil for Gaetano. Nico shoved a hand through his hair. He could handle it. He'd always been able to handle it. He would do so now, and he would send Miss Lily Morgan back to America where she belonged.

Madonna diavola, this was also not the first time he'd been presented with a paternity claim—though he'd never been presented with it in quite this way. Lily hadn't mentioned the child at all until he'd shown her the picture. And then she'd been desperate to get the photo from him, had never actually come out and said the child was his. But it *must* be her intention. What else?

He lifted the photo, studied it—and felt that jolt of awareness and recognition he'd never experienced before. Unlike the children that two of his former lovers had tried to assert were his—each incident had been disproved and the claims retracted, though Nico still gave money for the children's care since it was not their faults they'd been born without fathers— this boy had the look of a Cavelli. It was more than the eyes— something in the dark curls, the smooth olive skin, the shape of jaw and nose, the firm set—even in a toddler—of the lips. The likeness was remarkable, yet surely it was a trick.

He'd been captivated by her, he remembered it well, but not so captivated he'd forgotten to take precautions when he'd made love to her. He never forgot to take precautions. It was as necessary to his existence as sleeping or eating. He'd grown up the product of an indiscretion, and he would not ever cause a child to suffer the way he had. When he had children, they would be legitimate, wanted, and loved.

But what if those precautions had somehow failed? Was it possible? Could he be this boy's father? And, if he was, how could she have kept him from his son for all this time?

But no, it was not possible. He would have remembered if something happened to the condom; nothing had. The child could not be his, no matter how strong the likeness. It was a photographic trick.

Satisfied, he dropped the photo into a potted plant. He would not be played for a fool by this woman. Soon, he would know the truth. And tonight he would formalize his engagement to Princess Antonella, would move forward with the effort to unite Montebianco and Monteverde by honoring the commitment his family had made to the Romanellis when Gaetano was still alive. Antonella Romanelli was a beautiful woman; surely he would be well pleased with her as his wife.

Nico turned from the view and strode toward the terrace doors. He only took a few steps before faltering. With a muttered curse, he retrieved the picture and tucked it against his heart.

CHAPTER TWO

LILY BOLTED UPRIGHT on the musty cot, panic gripping her. Where was she? Why was she so cold?

A moment later, she remembered. The thin blanket she'd huddled under just wasn't enough protection. She scrubbed both her hands through her hair and got to her feet, hugging herself against the chill settling into the damp fortress walls as night crept over the city. How had she managed to fall asleep after her encounter with Nico?

Her eyes were gritty and tired, and her head throbbed. She'd cried so hard she'd given herself a migraine, though it was thankfully nothing more than a dull pain now. The sleep had helped at least.

The sudden clanging of the metal door in the passageway startled a little cry from her. Her heart pounded as she backed toward the opposite wall of the cell. A naked bulb overhead gave off only meager light and she squinted into the darkness outside the bars. A big shape shuffled into view and thrust a key into the lock. The door swung open just as she made out the uniform of a Montebiancan police officer.

"Come with me, *signorina*," the man said in thick English.

"Where are you taking me?" Fear, sharp and cold, slashed into her. Did the prince plan to have her thrown off a cliff somewhere?

Stop being silly.

"Come," he said, motioning. She hesitated only a moment longer, deciding she might have a better chance once she was out of this cell. She could give him the slip if the opportunity presented itself, or perhaps she could scream for help. It wasn't much of a plan, but it was better than sitting here another night.

The policeman ushered her up into the bright light of the rooms above the ancient cells. Before she could grow accustomed to the light, she was outside in the cool night air. A Mercedes limo idled near the exit and a man in a dark chauffeur's uniform snapped the car door open.

Lily faltered. The policeman held out his hand, motioning at the car. "Please," he said.

She hesitated, glancing at the street beyond the black iron gates. There was no escape that way, so she climbed into the car, her mind racing with possibilities. The door slammed behind her and a moment later the car whisked into traffic. Her questions about where they were going didn't penetrate the glass between her and the driver, so she settled into the plush leather of the interior and watched the city lights slide by as she planned her escape.

Lily gripped the door handle in a damp palm, her heart racing. When the car came to a halt at a light, she pulled, intending to slip out and disappear into the night before the driver could blink—but the door was locked. She jerked it again and again, but it refused to open. The driver didn't even glance at her. The car started moving, climbing steadily uphill, and Lily bit her lip, tears of frustration choking her.

Soon, they passed beneath an archway and into a courtyard. The car came to a halt. Lily pulled in a deep breath as her door swung open. Whatever was about to happen, she would *not* be a blubbering wreck. She was stronger than her fear, stronger than Nico Cavelli could ever imagine. She'd had to be.

A man in a colorful palace uniform beckoned her. Only then did it dawn on her that they'd arrived at the Cavelli Palace. The Moorish fortress sat at the highest point of the city, its white walls gleaming in both sun and moonlight. It commanded sweeping views of the sea and sparkled like a diamond in the center of a pendant. She'd gazed at it for two days, wondering if Nico was here, what he was doing, if he ever thought of her.

She'd certainly gotten her answer, hadn't she?

She was hurried through a door and down a series of corridors, finally arriving at closed gilt double doors. The palace guard rapped and spoke in Italian. A moment later, a voice answered and the doors swung open.

Blood rushed to Lily's head as she crossed the threshold. The room was a confection of ornate Moorish arches, mosaics, antiques, priceless artwork and tapestries. The gilt alone could pay for Danny's college tuition wherever he chose to go. A massive crystal chandelier threw glittering light into every corner. Her senses were overwhelmed as she tried to take it all in.

The doors clicked shut behind her and she whirled, her gaze colliding with that of the man walking in from an adjoining room.

If he wanted to intimidate her, he was doing a fine job. He was tall and broad, his body encased in a glittering uniform that surprised her with its ornate formality. A red sash crossed from his right shoulder to his waist. The uniform was dark, black or navy, and studded with gold. Medals draped across his chest in a colorful row of ribbons and polished silver discs and stars. A saber, dripping with tassels, was strapped to his side.

He lifted his hands and peeled off first one white glove and then the other while she gaped. He tossed them onto a chair with the hat she hadn't noticed before.

Desperately, Lily tried to conjure the image of the somewhat shaggy-haired student she'd thought him to be in New Orleans. He'd smiled a lot then. Laughed. How could this person be the same? Did he have a twin, perhaps? A twin who'd given her a false name?

For once, she wished she'd read more about him. Her knowledge was limited to gossip magazines and celebrity Web sites. She'd steadfastly refused to find out anything more once she'd discovered just how colossal a mistake in judgment she'd made. What good would it have done to pore over his biography when she was never going to see him again? Lily Morgan dating a prince—yeah, that was freaking hilarious.

"This is what is going to happen," he said coolly. "You are going to answer me truthfully and completely, and then you will call your friend Carla—"

"I want to call her now," Lily said firmly, only mildly surprised he knew her best friend's name. He'd been busy the last few hours, that's for sure. "She must be frantic with worry, and I want to know my son is well."

Nico held up a hand. "All in good time, *signorina*. First, you answer my question, and then you call."

Lily was tired and achy from too little sleep and the cold prison cell, and her head still throbbed dully. Her temper was on its last thread, and she no longer cared if she was talking to a prince or not. He put his pants on the same way as everyone else—not to mention he'd once deigned to sleep with her—so that gave her as good a reason as any to speak to him as an equal. "I'm calling her now, or I'm not answering."

Nico's eyes gleamed with suppressed annoyance. "You do not wish to test me, *signorina*. Your position is precarious enough, do you not think?"

Lily's chin nudged up a notch. "What do you plan to do, throw me back in that dungeon?"

"Perhaps. Trafficking in stolen antiquities is a significant crime in Montebianco. We take our heritage very seriously here."

Lily's right temple pounded. "I didn't steal anything. If you check with the street vendor, you'll know it's the truth."

"We are having some difficulty locating him. Not to mention that street vendors do not typically sell priceless artworks as if they are cheap trinkets."

"You're lying." The man had a stall in the market, for goodness' sake. How hard was it to find him again?

"I assure you I am not. He seems to have disappeared. If ever he was there in the first place."

Lily's bravado leached away under the weight of his arrogant surety. She was too tired to fight him, and too worried about her son to care about matching wits with this cold-blooded man any longer. She just wanted it over with. "Fine— what do you want to know?"

"I want you to tell me if this child is mine."

Lily's lungs refused to work properly. Liquid fear softened her spine, her knees, but somehow she remained upright. "What kind of question is that?" she asked on little more than a whisper.

His eyes flashed fire. "It is the kind of question you will answer truthfully if you wish to remain free."

She nearly choked. "You call this free?"

"Lily," he said, a hint of exasperation in his voice. And something else. Pain? Weariness?

She swallowed, dropped her gaze to study the tiles at her feet. Her heart pounded so hard she felt dizzy. It was the moment of truth, the one she'd never thought would come. Would he somehow care for her and Danny? Would he help them, be a father to her boy?

Of course he wouldn't. He was marrying a princess, God help the poor woman, and he wasn't about to change his ways just because he had yet another illegitimate child in this world. He might give her money to take care of Danny, but Lily knew that everything came with a price. She'd basically taken care of herself since she was fifteen years old, and she would continue to take care of herself and Danny on the strength of her will and determination. She would not accept handouts from Nico.

A finger under her chin tipped her head up. She hadn't realized he'd moved so close. The touch stung, brought memories to the surface she'd rather forget. His eyes were mesmerizing, as pale and blue as a winter lake. She'd wanted to drown in them once. Wanted to drown in him.

Part of her still did.

"Why does it matter?" she said, fighting a wave of panic.

His gaze never wavered, piercing her to the core. The contrast of his soft words was jarring to her senses. "Is this boy mine?"

In a split second, a million possible outcomes crossed her mind. And yet there was only one answer she could give, no matter how it tortured her to do so. "Yes," she whispered.

She was utterly still as his hand dropped. A moment later, while time stood still, he twirled a lock of her hair around his finger. "I remember this hair," he said softly. "It is still like the finest silk in my hands."

He'd moved closer than she'd realized, his body mere fractions away. The hilt of his sword grazed her beneath the ribs. "You remember?" she said, then cursed herself for sounding so desperate for an affirmative answer.

His gaze dropped to her mouth, lingered long enough that warmth blossomed between her thighs. Had she ever been kissed so thoroughly as when he'd kissed her? She stared at his lips, remembering the first brush of them. Remembering how his tongue dipped in to stroke her own, the way she'd sighed and opened to him, the utter rush of desire that flooded her as the kiss deepened into something that left them both gasping for breath and sanity when it was through.

He smelled so good, like citrus and spice and warm Mediterranean nights. She wanted to lean into him, wanted to kiss him again, wanted to know if what she'd felt with him had been real or a fluke.

"I remember you," he said. For an insane moment she thought he might really kiss her. With a soft curse, he moved away, unstrapping the sword as he walked. It clattered to the floor beside the chair with the rest of his gear before he spun and fixed her with a glare.

"I remember that we met in Jackson Square when a pick-pocket tried to steal your purse. I remember meeting you for three nights in a row in front of the cathedral. But most of all, I remember the last night. Mardi Gras. You were still a virgin."

Lily didn't care if she had permission or not. She moved to a plush couch and sank down on it, aware that she hadn't showered since yesterday and that she probably smelled as musty as the dungeon. But her legs wouldn't hold her up any longer.

"But when you came to the prison…" Her voice trailed off as she thought about how cold and cruel he would have to be to put her through that ordeal earlier. This was not a man to lose her head over, not a fairy-tale prince on a white stallion. This was a petty, privileged man who didn't care about anything but his own pleasure.

"This is what you will do now," he continued. "You will call your friend Carla and have her bring the boy to the airport. She will turn him over to a woman in my employ. Her name is Gisela—"

"No!" Lily shot to her feet. "I'm not telling Carla to give my son to a stranger—"

"*Our* son, is he not, Lily?"

Her heart battered her ribs. She would not lose her baby to this man! "Surely you can't be prepared to take my word on it," she flung at him with far more bravado than she felt. "Let me go home and you'll never hear another thing from me, I swear."

"That I cannot do, *signorina*." Irritation crossed his features as he stalked toward her again. "And I already know the truth. Our son was born nearly seventeen months ago, on November the twenty-fifth, in a small hospital in Port Pierre, Louisiana. You were in labor for twenty-two hours, and the only person at your bedside was Carla Breaux."

Lily sank onto the couch again as her legs gave way. *He knew the truth.* "Why did you ask me if he was yours if you know so much?"

"Because I wanted to hear you say it."

Lily felt as if she were collapsing in on herself. Her body folded over, slowly, until her head was nearly between her knees. Fury and fear mingled in her gut, bubbled into a great howl of rage that erupted from her throat, astonishing her.

Astonishing Nico, if the alarm on his face was any indication.

"You are *not* taking my baby away from me," she vowed. "I'll go back to that cell and stay there, but I will *not* tell Carla to hand over Danny to you."

He went to the bar set against one wall and poured a measure of caramel-colored liquid into a glass. Then he returned and held the cut crystal out to her. "Drink this."

"No."

"You are overwrought. This will help."

She gripped the glass in both hands, more to make him go away than anything. When he stood so close, her head felt fuzzy. Thankfully, he retreated a few steps. He picked up a phone, issued what she assumed were a set of orders since whoever was on the other end never had time to speak before he hung up again.

"You will call your friend Carla and tell her to bring Daniele to the airport tomorrow morning."

"I won't," she said quietly, resenting the way he so easily Italianized her son's name.

"Indeed you will," Nico replied. "You can make this easy, or you can make it hard. Should you not cooperate, you might never see Daniele again. Because you will not leave Montebianco. He could grow up motherless, and alone."

Numbness crept over her. "You would do that to your own son? You would deny him his mother?"

She didn't miss the nearly imperceptible clenching of his jaw. "I will do what it takes to make you see reason, *cara*. If you cooperate, this will not have to happen, *si?*"

"How can you be so cruel?"

He shrugged an elegant shoulder, and Lily saw red. The spoiled bastard! The glass tumbled to the floor and shattered against the tile as she lunged for him. Nico was faster, however. He swept her high into his arms and carried her across the room as she kicked and struggled.

"*Dio,* woman, you are wearing sandals. Do you want to slice your feet to ribbons?"

Lily didn't care. She simply didn't care about anything any longer. This man, this cold evil man, was trying to take away the one person in the world who meant the most to her. It was her greatest fear come to life. She would not allow it.

She twisted in his iron grip, throwing him off balance so that he stumbled. Lily pressed her advantage and they fell to the thick Oriental carpet together, Nico taking the brunt of the impact. A moment later, he flipped her and she found herself on her back, Nico's hard form pressing into her, breast to belly to hip.

"Stop fighting me, *cara,*" he said harshly. "It changes nothing."

Lily wiggled beneath him, tried to shake him off. His solid form didn't budge. The point of a star-shaped medal dug into her ribs. "Why are you doing this to me?" she cried. "You have dozens of children with your mistresses, so why do you care about mine?"

Rage, disbelief, frustration—they chased across his face in equal measure. "I have one child, Liliana. Only one. And you have kept him from me."

"I don't believe you," she gasped out.

Nico shifted and the medal's point thankfully stopped pricking her. He gripped her arms, forced them above her head. He seemed to hover on the edge of control. "Have you never thought that gossip magazines might lie?"

"They can't all be lies." There had to be a grain of truth, right? Perhaps they exaggerated, but there must be something to it. Not one of the reporters she knew at the *Register* would dare write something so patently false.

Nico's laugh was short and bitter. "You have obviously never been the victim of these carrion. They feed on outrage and misdirection. There's hardly a single thing they print about me that is true."

"Now I know you're lying. I've seen photos of you with lots of women—"

"I have had many mistresses," he said, cutting her off. "This is to be expected—"

"Why? Because you're some kind of God's gift—"

"*Basta!* You seek to exasperate me, *signorina,* and you succeed. Nevertheless, I have *one* child."

Lily's chest heaved in frustration as she stared up at him. But her eyes closed as the truth of his words sank in. Gossip magazines thrived on scandal. She knew that. But she didn't want to believe he spoke the truth. Because if he did, so much she'd thought about him would be wrong. The blood drained from her head as the implications sank in.

"But if Danny really is the only one, that would mean—"

She couldn't finish the sentence, uncertain what to say next. Was Danny in line for a throne? *Impossible.*

Nico said it for her. "Yes, *cara,* our child is my heir and second in line to the throne of Montebianco."

Her insides were jelly. "How is that possible?" she managed. "We aren't even married."

"It just is," he said, his accent thickening suddenly as she moved.

Lily took advantage of his distraction to try and buck him off. She arched her back and flexed her body upward, shoving into the cradle of his hips. His arousal sent a jolt of sensation sizzling through her.

In spite of her anger and frustration, the feeling was delicious. Dangerous.

Nico's breath caught as she shoved against him. The sound was slight, but she heard it nonetheless.

And just like that she was on fire, absolutely aflame with longing. How could it be possible? How could she feel sexual desire for him when he wanted to ruin her life? He'd given her the most precious thing in her world, and now he wanted to take it away. And her body didn't seem to care. She redoubled her efforts to throw him off.

"Maledizione," he ground out between clenched teeth. "Stop moving—or would you like to take this into the bedroom and do it properly?"

Lily's palms pushed against the crisp material of his uniform. A desperate, greedy part of her did indeed want to *do it properly.* But her common sense, her anger, her sheer dislike of the man won out. "Get off me."

"As you wish," he said, then bounded up and left her to climb to her feet alone.

Lily hugged herself, her body still tingling with the shock

of desire. How could she want him? She closed her eyes, squeezed her arms tight around her middle. My God, she really was her mother's daughter.

She could not afford the distraction of such thoughts. She had to focus. "What now?"

He whirled on her, his uniform as crisp and perfect as if he hadn't just been rolling on the floor with her. His royal bearing was absolute. She wondered that she'd never noticed it in the three days she'd spent with him in New Orleans.

"You will call your friend and instruct her to turn over the child."

Lily shook her head. "Why? So you can marry your princess and raise my child with her? Not just no, but hell no."

Nico's brows drew together. "We will need to work on that mouth of yours. It's unfit for a royal."

Lily snorted. "But not unfit enough for you two years ago when you seduced me, huh? Go to hell, Nico," she said, stressing his name without the title.

"You most definitely require etiquette lessons, *cara mia.*" His gaze raked her from head to toe. "And a suitable wardrobe."

Lily stiffened. Her clothes might not be the height of fashion, but they were usually clean and neat. Unlike now, when she'd spent the last twenty-four hours in a prison cell and just wrestled on the floor with a prince.

Nico retrieved a cell phone from a table. "You and your son will never want for anything again. You will no longer have to work. I will take care of you both."

Lily stared at the gleaming phone held so casually in his hand, his words more seductive than she cared to admit. Never to have to struggle again? Never have to worry about keeping her apartment or her health insurance? Money and freedom from the fear of not having enough to take care of her baby?

But no. What was he offering her—the chance to be a kept woman while he married his princess and had babies with her?

She'd work herself half to death before she accepted such treatment. She'd taken care of Danny this long; she could continue to do so just fine on her own.

"I can take care of my son without you," she said.

His expression grew so chilly she had to suppress a shiver. "Apparently I have not expressed myself in a manner you understand. There is no choice, Liliana. You and the boy belong to me."

Lily snorted. "Even you can't own people, Nico."

He merely smiled at her. A frisson of warning raced down her spine and pooled in her belly. A moment later, he lifted the phone to his ear and began speaking in Italian. This time, it was a conversation, not simply a set of orders. When he finished, he laid the phone on a nearby table.

"What did you do?"

His self-satisfied smile did nothing to ease her tension. "Five million dollars is a lot of money, no? Do you think your friend will turn this down for you?"

Black spots swam before her eyes, but Lily refused to buckle. "My God…"

"*Si*, it is not likely, is it?" He moved closer, shadowing her like the predator he was, impossibly male and utterly beautiful in spite of the hatred she felt for him in that moment. "She will not turn it down, Liliana. Shall I tell you why?"

When she didn't reply, he continued, "Carla has a boyfriend with a little problem. He likes the game tables in New Orleans a bit too much, yes? He has taken much from her in the last three years. Her savings are gone, her house leveraged in excess of its current value. This money represents a new life, *cara mia*. She will not say no."

Lily blinked up at him. She knew she was defeated. Carla hadn't told her the extent of Alan's problems, but Lily had known that it worried her. Carla was almost as bad as her own mother when it came to her slavish devotion to a man who cared more for himself than for her.

His fingers stroked down her cheek, impossibly tender when compared with his actions. She shuddered in spite of her vow not to react. "What do you plan to do with my baby?"

His eyes hardened, his hand dropping away. "*Our* baby, Liliana."

Lily faced him squarely, ready to do battle, heartsick and heartbroken all at once. "You can't buy me off, too, Nico. I will never leave Danny with you willingly."

"Clearly not," he said, his voice deepening with anger. "But you will not need to do so."

Lily gaped at him. "My God, you *are* unbelievable—how do you think your wife-to-be is going to feel about me and Danny, huh?"

"Why don't you ask her yourself?"

"What? Are you insane?"

Nico grabbed her by the arm and propelled her toward the opposite wall, her puny resistance not slowing him in the least. He approached a door, and for one crazy minute she thought it was a bedroom and there was a woman inside. He would throw open the door and there she would be, the Princess Antonella Romanelli of Monteverde, a black-haired gray-eyed beauty, sprawled across silk sheets and pouting prettily because her lover was taking too long to get the *baby mama* under control.

Abruptly, they slammed to a halt, Nico pivoting behind her, the full length of his body pressing into her. She tried to jerk away, but he gripped her chin—more gently than she expected—and forced her head forward.

Lily gasped. "Is this a joke?"

She stared at her reflection—their reflection—in the mirror. The darkness of his fingers against her skin, her hair wild and tumbling around her shoulders in a silky mess. Her pink cotton shirt was stained over her left shoulder, and her eyes, though tired, gleamed with fury. Nico, in contrast, was cool and unruffled. If not for his quickened heartbeat against her, she'd almost think him bored.

But no, there it was, that flash of something in his eyes, in the set of his jaw, that spoke volumes without a sound being uttered.

"No joke, Liliana. I have broken a long-sought-after treaty between my country and Monteverde, not to mention embarrassed my father and our allies, so that I can do what should have been done the instant you conceived my child."

"I—I don't understand," she whispered, searching his face in the mirror, her heart slamming into her ribs.

"Of course you do," he replied, dipping his head until his lips almost grazed the shell of her ear. Almost, but not quite.

"You, Miss Lily Morgan, are about to become the Crown Princess, my consort, and the mother of my children."

CHAPTER THREE

SHE LOOKED UTTERLY STUNNED. Not that he blamed her; he was still somewhat stunned himself. He had a son with this woman, a fact that had the power to punch him in the solar plexus and leave him gasping for breath every time he thought of it.

A son she'd kept secret from him. The electric current zapping through him as he pressed against her was most certainly rage, nothing more.

"You can't be serious," she finally squeaked out. Her green eyes were huge as she blinked at him in disbelief. The platinum color of her hair made her almost ethereal. Surely, this is what had attracted him to her in the first place. That and the fact she'd been blissfully unaware of his identity. The experience was so novel that he'd quite possibly been more attracted to her than he would have otherwise been. She'd treated him like an ordinary person and he'd found it refreshing.

"I am indeed serious, Liliana." He'd gotten his answer in the moments before he'd left his quarters to attend the State dinner. His investigators worked remarkably fast, and what they'd turned up was evidence he could not ignore. She'd given birth almost nine months to the day from the night he'd made love to her. She could have found another lover right away, true, but the child's resemblance to him was too strong to discount. He would of course take the official step of verifying the child's parentage, but it was merely a formality at this point.

When he considered how he'd missed the first seventeen months of his boy's life, how this woman had kept his son from him, he wanted to shake her and demand to know how she could do such a thing. He let her go before the urge overwhelmed him and took a step away.

He would marry her because his personal code of honor would permit nothing less. It was his duty. But he didn't have to like it. Or her.

She spun around to face him. "B-but I'm not a princess, I don't know how to be a prin—"

"You will learn," he said harshly. She wasn't the ideal bride for him, but she could be trained. She was attractive enough, and she'd already proven she had the moxie required to stand up beneath the pressure. When she was coiffed and dressed appropriately, she would no longer appear so common. She was not as beautiful as Antonella, but she was quite lovely in a natural way. Antonella didn't affect him one way or the other. He could take or leave the Monteverdian princess.

But Lily—

Nico crossed to the bar and poured another cognac. This time he downed the liquid himself, welcomed the burn of fine Montebiancan brandy. *Per Dio,* it'd been a hell of a night thus far. And he wasn't finished fighting with himself.

Part of him, a mad and primal part of him, was so completely aware of the woman across the room that he wanted to haul her to his bed and strip her slowly before burying himself inside her for the rest of the night.

Madness. Sheer madness. The urge filled him with both hunger and rage, and he worked to force it down deep and put a lid on it.

In the two months since Gaetano had died, he'd mostly ignored the sensual side of his nature as he'd worked to further

Montebiancan interests and be the kind of heir to the throne that his people deserved. He was sorely regretting the lack at the moment. It made Lily Morgan seem far more irresistible to him than she should be.

"Surely we can work this out another way," she said, her voice small and hesitant. "You can have visitation and—"

"Visitation," he exclaimed, slicing her words off before she could finish. He shrugged out of the sash and tossed it aside, then worked the buttons of his uniform jacket with one hand, throwing it open with an angry gesture to let the air from the terrace door he'd left ajar cool his body. This night had thrown him so far out of balance that he half wondered if he would ever recover his equilibrium. "You are quite lucky this is no longer the Middle Ages, Liliana. As it is, you are getting far more from me than you deserve."

If he thought she would be chastened by his words, he was in for a surprise. She lit up like a firecracker. *Dio,* she was lovely. And she'd just cost him five million dollars, a trade treaty with a neighboring kingdom, and every last shred of credibility he'd built since becoming the Crown Prince. Being illegitimate, and having the playboy reputation he'd had before his brother's death, he'd had to work doubly hard to prove himself.

Now, all his effort lay in tatters around him. The thought fueled the anger roiling in his gut.

"More than I deserve?" she said, her voice not small any longer but large and strong. "How dare you! I've been on my own for these two years, enduring what you could not begin to imagine in your ivory tower, taking care of a baby and—"

"Silence!" There was no way on this earth he would listen to her berate him for what had been essentially her decision to keep him in the dark about their child. She would pay for what she'd done. He was far too angry, far too close to losing the last shred of his control. "If you are aware of what is good for you, *cara,* you will not speak of this any further tonight."

She opened her mouth, and he slapped the crystal on the table and moved toward her. When she scurried backward, her eyes widening, he checked his progress. He was on the edge of emotions he'd never felt before, torn between wanting to protect and destroy, and it made him reckless.

He snatched up the phone and pressed the button that would summon his housekeeper. When he put it down, Lily was chewing her lip, arms folded beneath her breasts as if to protect herself. Or to keep warm. The night was probably cooler than she was accustomed to in her native Louisiana. A tremor passed over her, confirming his observation. Beneath her shirt, her nipples peaked, small and tight, and goose bumps rose on her skin.

Nico swallowed, remembering how perfect her breasts had been when he'd first bared them to his sight. How responsive she'd been as she'd moaned and clutched his shoulders when he kissed the tight little points.

Dio, *this was insane.*

Nico shook the memories away and peeled off his jacket. "You are cold," he said as he closed the distance between them. "Take this, *cara.*"

He placed the jacket on her shoulders and she clutched the material around her, thanking him softly. He turned his back on her and moved away.

He heard the intake of her breath, braced himself for what she might say next—but there was only silence.

Finally, she spoke. "Nico, I'm sorry that—"

The door opened and the housekeeper entered, interrupting whatever she'd been about to say. Nico didn't look at her again.

"Please show our guest to her room," he told the woman awaiting his instructions. "And send someone to clean up the broken glass."

Signora Mazetti gave a short bow and waited for Lily to

join her. Out of the corner of his eye, he saw Lily remove the jacket and place it carefully over the back of the settee closest to her. Then she followed the housekeeper without complaint.

Lily awoke to the sound of china and silverware delicately clinking together. She sat up, yawning, and blinked as she tried to take in her surroundings. Brocade curtains hung from a canopy and were drawn back to let light filter into the giant bed. For a moment, she thought she'd been upgraded to the best suite the hotel had—but then she remembered.

She was in the palace, in Prince Nico's apartment. If you could call a wing of a royal palace an apartment. And she was as much a prisoner here as she'd been in the dungeon cell of the old fortress.

A woman in uniform stood off to one side, fussing with a tray. She turned and dropped a curtsy before coming forward and settling the tray laden with bone china and thick silverware across Lily's lap.

"His Highness says you are to eat and dress, *signorina*. He wishes you to join him in precisely one hour."

The woman curtsied again and slipped out the door, closing it behind her. Lily started to set the tray aside, but the scents of coffee and food wafted up to her, reminding her how hungry she was. She'd been unable to eat during the twenty-four hours she'd spent in prison. Last night, all she'd wanted was to shower and sleep—but now her stomach rumbled insistently.

She thought about tossing on her clothes and trying to find a phone—maybe she could call Carla and explain she was being held against her will. Or maybe she could call her boss and tell him she'd been kidnapped. She'd call the consulate herself except she couldn't waste precious time looking for the phone number. *Someone* would help her, she was positive.

Her suitcase had arrived, but her laptop, cell phone and passport had not been returned, naturally. Nico had cut off not only her contact with the outside world, but also any chance of escape. But Lily Morgan did not give up so easily, damn him.

Her stomach growled so hard it hurt, and she had to acknowledge that if she didn't eat something now she wouldn't get very far. Lily wolfed down the fresh bread and thinly sliced meats and cheeses along with a soft-boiled egg and two cups of strong coffee with cream.

Half an hour later, after she'd showered again and dressed in jeans and a T-shirt, she tried the door. It was unlocked and she slipped into the corridor, looking right and left. Which direction had she come from last night? She couldn't remember, so she started down the hall and tried doors. When she emerged into the living room where Nico had coldly informed her she would be his wife, she stumbled to a halt, a shocked "Oh" escaping her. With bright sunlight spearing through the windows and through the terrace doors, the room glittered with gold and colored glass mosaic.

She dragged her gaze from the opulence of the room and searched for a phone, finally finding it on an inlaid cherry-wood table beside one of the velvet couches. Lily snatched it from the cradle, not sure who she should call first.

"You have to go through the palace operator, I'm afraid."

Lily jumped and slammed the phone back down. Nico stood across from her, a newspaper in one hand, a cup in the other. He was so tall and elegant. She didn't usually think of men as elegant, but Nico was. Elegant, gorgeous and so masculine he shot her pulse through the stratosphere just looking at him.

He wore a dark gray suit that was clearly worth more money than she'd ever made in six months of work. The fabric looked beyond expensive, perfectly tailored. He also wore a crisp white shirt with no tie, and black loafers. A ruby signet ring glittered on his right hand.

"I want my phone back."

"You will have a new phone, Lily. And many other things besides." His gaze raked her from head to toe and she bit the inside of her lip. No doubt he saw a poor raga-muffin, a woman unfit to be a princess, and was disappointed. Well, by God, she *was* unfit to be a princess. Nor did she want to be one. She would never, ever fit in here. It was preposterous.

Lily thrust her chin in the air. "I've reconsidered your offer," she said. "You can visit Danny whenever you like, and I will bring him to Montebianco often, but it's impossible for me to marry you. We'll just have to manage another way."

"Manage?" He set the cup and paper down and came over to where she stood, looming above her. He seemed surprised—or maybe he was amused—but quickly masked it with his trademark arrogance. "You have misunderstood once again, Liliana. There was no offer. There is simply what will be."

"You can't possibly want to marry me," she said softly, staring up at him with her heart thudding into her throat. Did he have to be so darn breathtaking?

"What I want is of no consequence."

"It's not what *I* want."

"Perhaps you should have thought of that two years ago."

Lily blew out a breath. "I don't think either of us was thinking much that night, were we?"

A muscle in Nico's jaw ticked as he watched her. "Clearly not. But what about after, Lily? What about when you learned you were pregnant?"

She studied her clasped hands, suddenly unable to look at him. "I didn't know who you really were."

"But you found out. Why did you not contact me then?" His voice was controlled, as if he were struggling with his temper.

Lily put distance between them, instinctively wrapping her arms around herself. How could she tell him she'd been afraid? Afraid he would take her baby away and paradoxically afraid he'd be the kind of father she'd had growing up? Instead, she focused on the one truth that was easily explainable. "Assuming I could have figured out how to get past the layers between you and the public, would you have believed me?"

"Eventually."

Lily bit back a bitter laugh. "Oh yes, how lovely *that* would have been."

Nico sliced a hand through the air, as if cutting through their conversation. "None of this is important now. What is important is that you *still* had no plan to inform me. Had you not found yourself detained here, I would never know of our son's existence, would I?"

"No," Lily said quietly, forcing herself to meet his gaze.

Nico's eyes hardened. "Trust me, *cara*, if there were another way, I would send you far from Montebianco and never see your deceitful face again. As it is, I think we shall have to make do with the situation, *si?*"

"I'm deceitful?" she said, her voice rising. "*Me?* What about you? Not only did you fail to tell me you were really a prince, but you also seem to have forgotten you were supposed to meet me in front of the cathedral—"

"I was called back to Montebianco unexpectedly," he cut in, his voice rising to match hers. "I sent someone to inform you."

"I didn't get the message."

His expression didn't change. "You have only yourself to blame. When my man was unable to find you, I sent out inquiries. Had I known your real name was Margaret, I might have been able to contact you."

Lily bit down on her bottom lip, surprised at how quickly she found herself on the verge of angry tears. She would *not* allow this man to affect her so strongly. Not now. It was too late to discuss what-ifs.

"I've always gone by my middle name. Why would I have told you my legal name as if you were a prospective employer or something? It simply didn't occur to me."

She shook her head. Wasn't it just the story of her life to have something so vital hinge on something as simple as a legal name? "I don't want to be unhappy. I don't think you want to be unhappy, either. And if you force me to marry you, we will both be miserable. You have to see this is true, right?"

"It is too late for that," he said harshly.

Lily tried to sound reasonable. "Why? You could still marry your princess and have children with her. And how can Danny be in line for the throne anyway? Don't princes have to be born legitimate?"

Nico's face was a stone mask. "In Montebianco, royal is royal."

"I don't want this for my child," Lily insisted. "I want him to grow up normal." The wealth frightened her. And not only Nico's wealth, but the atmosphere he lived in. How could Danny be anything but spoiled rotten if he grew up here? How could he become a decent young man, and not a womanizing lothario like the prince standing before her? It terrified her, the thought her boy would be lost to her once he arrived. And that he would become the kind of man she despised most.

Oh God, how could she be tied to a playboy prince for life? Because no matter that she was the only woman he'd ever gotten pregnant—and it must be true considering the lengths he was going to in order to keep her here—he was still the worst sort of Casanova. Would she become just like her mother, desperate for one man's affections and willing to put up with whatever he dished out just to be with him?

Worse, would Nico be a fair-weather father?

"He is *our* child, Lily. You have already tried to deprive him of his birthright with your selfishness."

She blinked. Selfish? Was she? Was it possible?

"That's not true," she said. She sounded defensive to her own ears. And perhaps a bit guilty. In protecting her baby, had she really been trying to keep him all to herself? Had she really been afraid Nico would take him away? Or had her motives been purely because she'd believed he was not the kind of man who could be a good father?

"You will do so no longer," Nico continued. "Daniele is my son and I *will* be his father in truth from this moment forward. If you expect to remain in his life, then you will stand before the authorities and agree to be my wife. That is your choice, Lily."

"That's not a choice," she said, her throat aching with the effort to speak normally. "It's a command."

Nico's gaze was unreadable. "Then perhaps we finally understand one another."

When Nico had said she needed a suitable wardrobe, Lily hadn't realized he'd meant to fly her to Paris to visit couture shops that very afternoon. While they were winging their way to France, he'd finally let her call her boss and explain that she wouldn't be back at work tomorrow as planned.

Hell, she wouldn't be back at all it appeared, though she didn't say that. Darrell was curious, but Lily had no words to explain what had happened. She assured him she was safe, said she would e-mail him her impressions of Montebianco along with the photos she'd taken, and ended the call.

Then she looked over at Nico. He was typing something

on his laptop. "I need to use a computer," she said firmly. "I have a job to finish."

"All in good time, Lily." He didn't look up.

She tried to keep her cool as she explained. "The paper paid my way here and they expect me to finish the job. I can't leave them high and dry."

This time, he did look at her. "Of course. But it can wait until we return to Montebianco, yes?"

"I'd prefer to work on it now."

He closed the lid of his laptop. "Did you not keep notes on your computer?"

"Of course I did. But the police confiscated it."

"It was turned over to me. You may have it back when we are in Montebianco. And then you may access your notes. Does this work for you?"

A current of frustration zapped through her. "Does it *work* for me? What you really mean is that I don't have a choice. Why not say so?"

He smiled, though it held no humor. "Your *choice, cara,* is to wait until we return to Montebianco or to use this laptop." He looked at his watch, glanced out the window. "However, you will need to work fast, as we will be landing very shortly."

Lily crossed her arms and looked away. She knew she'd been snappish, but she couldn't apologize. Not after all he'd put her through the last few hours. When she didn't say anything, he stowed the laptop; twenty minutes later, they were on the ground and exiting the plane.

Once they entered Paris, her black mood lifted a little. Seeing the Eiffel Tower as they drove through the streets was exciting. She wanted to see everything, to spend hours exploring the sights she'd only read about, but Nico informed her they did not have time for touring.

Instead, she was ushered in and out of Prada, Versace, Louboutin, Dior and Hermès—and those were only the names she remembered. She'd never seen such an array of expensive clothes and handbags in her life. Nor had she ever thought she'd own a single piece of clothing from any of them, never mind an entire wardrobe. It was overwhelming to see the bags and boxes piling up.

"Nico, this is ridiculous," she finally said as they drove to the next shop on his list. "No one needs this much stuff."

"*Principessas* do." He looked up from his paper, half-bored, and gazed at her coolly.

"*No* one does," she shot back. Why did he make her feel as if she was six years old?

He dropped the paper onto the leather seat of the Rolls-Royce with a sigh. "Principessa Liliana Cavelli must be as chic and polished as it is possible for any woman to be. She will be the envy of some, the bane of others, and always—" he held up a finger when she would have spoken "—always she must be elegant and beautiful and a proper representative for Montebianco. She will dine with kings and queens, ambassadors, heads of state, and yes, perhaps even her own American president."

Lily felt her eyes widen.

"She is the wife of the next king, and the mother to the king after him. She must look the part and she must never, ever bring shame to the Cavelli name—or to her son—by refusing to do so. It is about more than her own desires, after all. It is about duty and honor, and centuries' old tradition."

"But it seems so extravagant," she said defensively.

"It may appear so now, but you will witness the truth for yourself soon enough. And you would not thank me if I allowed you to be unprepared for the role."

Lily turned away. Damn him for making her feel petty—and over what? Hundreds of thousands of dollars in clothing, shoes, handbags, luggage, belts, scarves, coats and lacy underwear. How did he manage it?

She thought of Danny, of his adorable baby smile and the way his eyes lit up when she came home at the end of each day, and her heart filled with love. Because of this crazy turn of events, her baby would never go hungry, would never do without medicine or a roof over his head or the warmest clothes in winter. He was her entire world; for him, she would wear sackcloth and ashes—or Prada and Gucci.

She despised the idea of accepting so much from Nico— and yet she realized she had no choice. Lily vowed she would teach Danny that money did not make the man. He would not grow up as spoiled and selfish as his father. Somehow, she would make sure he understood.

They didn't speak again and he went back to reading his paper. Soon, she found herself seated in a posh salon with a team of women hovering over her and one of Nico's hulking security guards standing by in the corner—yet another reminder her life had changed drastically. Was she really at risk in a salon? Quite possibly, she supposed. What kind of life would this be, always looking over her shoulder and wondering if danger lurked close by?

A question to which there could be no answer.

Nico stated that he had business elsewhere and would return for her in a couple of hours.

In the salon, at least, she absolutely refused to allow anything to be done that she did not feel comfortable with. Clothes were one thing; they were impermanent, changeable. But her hair and makeup were another thing all together. Hair grew back, but she wasn't accepting a cut that wasn't *her.* Fortunately, the women were under no orders to transform her into something of Nico's design.

Once her hair had been washed and trimmed, it was wrapped in some sort of healing hair mask—or perhaps that was *masque* since she was in France—while two women gave her a pedicure and manicure. A trip to the nail salon had been a little indulgence of hers before she'd had Danny. Since he'd been born, she'd not been able to spare any money, and she'd forgotten how much she missed it.

When the women were finished and she sat with her hands under a portable dryer, her attention was caught by a woman entering the salon. She had an entourage, and she was easily the most elegant, coolly beautiful woman that Lily had ever seen. She carried a tiny Pomeranian dog in one arm. Sable hair hung halfway down her back, rippling like silk when she turned. Beneath her jacket, she wore a thin sweater that rested midthigh with skinny black jeans and vibrant red stilettos. Huge sunglasses looked chic on her, though they would certainly make Lily look like a bug.

That was the kind of woman Nico needed. The kind he wanted her to be. The thought was a little depressing.

The women in the salon flocked to the newcomer, made her comfortable, brought her a café and spoke to her in hushed whispers. A moment later, she was on her feet, striding purposefully toward Lily's chair.

She whipped off the dark glasses, her reddened eyes spearing Lily with a glare. "You are Liliana Morgan?"

"Uh, yes," Lily replied, too shocked to correct her name. And too horrified. She'd only seen a couple of pictures, but she recognized the woman standing over her so angrily.

"I," she said imperiously, "am Princess Antonella Romanelli. I believe you have stolen my fiancé."

Lily swallowed. Oh. Dear. God.

"I'm sorry," she said. "Truly I am." Did she explain everything to this woman? Keep her mouth shut and hope she would go away? What did one do when confronted by an angry princess?

Antonella propped a bejeweled hand on one lean hip. "Of all the places, yes? Here I am, running from Montebianco to soothe my wounded pride, and you appear. Could the world be any crueler?"

Surprisingly, her eyes filled with tears; Lily found herself reaching for the princess's arm almost without thought. But what could she say that would help?

Antonella shifted out of reach before Lily touched her. "I have a habit of chasing away prospective grooms."

She grabbed a tissue from a box on the table and dabbed at her nose. Her gaze moved over Lily, not rudely, but assessing. "How has he chosen you? What have you done to him? *Dio,* I do not see it," she said. "Surely a child is not enough to make a difference."

"I'm sorry for your pain, Your Highness," Lily said, smarting from the remark and feeling her temper rising in spite of the princess's obvious distress, "but not everyone is as privileged or as beautiful as you. And my son is none of your concern."

Antonella laughed, a sweet sound that had no humor in it. "Oh my dear girl, forgive me for insulting you, but you cannot know what you've cost me. You cannot know."

Before Lily could reply, the princess was striding across the room, snapping her fingers and speaking in rapid Italian. She took her dog from an assistant as her entourage regrouped and scrambled to follow her out the door.

Lily numbly watched her progress, a horrifying realization striking her—Princess Antonella was in love with Nico. Did that mean that Nico was in love with her, too?

By the time Lily was finished in the salon, she barely recognized herself. Once the treatment had been washed from her hair, it had been blown out into a sleek mass of shiny, silky platinum before being pulled back into an elegant ponytail. Though Lily was no stranger to cosmetics, with a baby to look after she didn't usually have the time or the money for more than a tube of lip gloss and mascara. Now, she'd been shown how to apply a hint of blush and eyeshadow to accent her natural features. Her lips were a pale pink, and her lashes were long and lush.

She'd been shown to a dressing room where a selection of clothing from today's excursion waited for her. She changed into the slim pencil skirt and white top with tiny pearl buttons down the front. A wide black belt, silk trench coat and sky-high patent pumps finished the ensemble. She rolled up her jeans and sweatshirt and shoved them into the oversize Fendi bag that sat on the cream damask chaise, then studied herself in the mirror.

Did she look like a princess? Maybe. She certainly looked more elegant than she ever had in her life.

But she still felt like Lily Morgan from the wrong side of town, the girl with a chain-smoking, hard-drinking mother and an absentee father. She thought of Princess Antonella, of her beauty and sadness, and felt like the worst kind of human being. She'd come between two people who were right for each other—worse, she was almost glad for it. When she thought of Nico holding his princess, kissing her...

Well, she just couldn't think of it, that's all.

Lily left the salon with the guard at her elbow, guiding her toward the idling Rolls under the awning a few feet away. They were almost to the car when a bright light flashed in her face. And then another and another.

The guard shielded her with his body, moving her forward the entire time as voices called to her in French and flashbulbs lit up the surrounding area like lightning. A second later, the car door opened and she was thrust inside. Her pulse was unsteady as she craned her neck to watch the scene disappear behind her.

"Put this on," a smooth voice said.

Lily spun around, her heart in her throat, to face Nico. She hadn't even known he was in the car. His gaze flicked over her. Was that approval she saw? Oddly enough, she wanted his approval. The thought was not a welcome one, and she dropped her head to look at her clasped hands, her heart refusing to beat normally.

"Lily," he said, and she realized he held out a box. After a moment's hesitation, she accepted it. She didn't bother to ask what it was; she simply opened the lid—and felt the blood draining from her head as she contemplated the sparkling ring.

"It's very big," she said. "A very pretty sapphire."

Nico grasped the box and tugged the ring free. "It is a diamond." He took her hand and slipped it onto her finger before she could protest. The ring was too big and twisted beneath the weight of the diamond. Nico frowned. "We will have it sized in Montebianco."

"I can't wear this," she said, horrified at the size and weight of the hunk of metal and rocks on her hand. A blue diamond? So blue it looked like a sapphire? How much did something like that cost? She didn't even want to think about it.

"This is your engagement ring. You will wear it."

Hurt and confusion cascaded through her as she searched his face. Was he thinking of Antonella? But his expression was emotionless.

Her gaze dropped to her hand and the strange weight on her finger. She'd envisioned shopping for rings someday with a man she loved, going from store to store and trying them on, searching for the perfect one. It would be a joyful thing they shared, not a chore or a duty. Or a command.

This ring was nothing like what she'd imagined her engagement ring would one day be.

"I don't like it," she said, then regretted it the instant their eyes met. His expression was bored, irritated. He did not care. If he'd told her it was a family heirloom, and he was expected to give it to his bride, at least she would have known this meant something to him. But no, he'd walked into a jeweler's—or sent someone, more like—and told them to bring him a rare, expensive ring. This was about status, not tradition, not their child, and certainly not about love.

What would he have chosen for Antonella?

No. She couldn't go there, she simply couldn't. Lily closed her eyes, breathed deeply.

"It's too late," he said. "No doubt someone has already rung the press to inform them I bought this ring. It cannot be taken back."

Lily stared at the diamond, its glittering mass like a huge neon sign of ownership. Everything between them would be very public, she realized. Every look, every gesture, every word. Everything he did was for the cameras. In the space of a day, her life had turned into a reality show. The paparazzi were already swarming, if the incident a few moments ago was any indication. Would she ever know a moment's happiness, aside from the time she spent with Danny?

"How did New Orleans happen?" she said softly, realizing how uncharacteristic it must have been for him. He moved in his own circles, not in hers. It was an anomaly that they'd even met.

Nico studied her. She thought she saw a glimmer of admiration in his eyes. But it was gone quickly and she decided she'd imagined it.

"My life was different then."

"So why me?" She wanted to know, especially now that she knew firsthand the world he came from. Had seen the kind of women he was linked with in the pages of magazines the world over. Women unlike her. Glamorous women, gorgeous women.

Women like Princess Antonella.

"Because you did not know my identity. I found it novel."

The truth was raw, like an open cut, and he'd just poured salt onto it. Of course she hadn't known him. She was from a small town in Louisiana, not a glamorous metropolis. Oh what a cliché she'd been. The country mouse in the big bad city. Everything about New Orleans was grand, and different than she was accustomed to. Clearly, it had affected her judgment. She'd allowed herself to be swept away by his attention and charm, and by the wild abandon of Mardi Gras.

"If not for Danny, I could wish we'd never met," she replied.

He shoved a hand through his hair, the gesture full of frustration and regret. "*Si,* I wish this, too. But it is too late now. You are the mother of my child. Nothing can change that."

No, nothing could. How he must hate her for forever dividing him from the woman he had chosen to marry. He'd as good as told her that he regretted everything about his brief relationship with her. He was marrying her for Danny, nothing more.

Lily turned her head, the landscape blurring as the Rolls glided toward the airport. This was not at all the way she'd imagined her life would turn out.

But for her son, she would endure. He deserved a father, and Nico seemed determined to be one. It was more than her own father had ever done for her. Jack Morgan had never fought to be in her life. He'd seen her more as an inconvenience when he'd been there. If she were truthful with herself, she'd often believed that each time he left, it was because of her. Because she'd been bad or unlovable.

She dashed her tears away before Nico noticed. She was a woman now; she knew it was never the child's fault when a parent left, and yet the memory still had the power to sadden her and make her feel inadequate. She would not ever allow Danny to suffer the same way she had.

The car snaked through heavy airport traffic, finally turning and making its way over the tarmac toward the Boeing 737 that sat with engines idling. The red carpet leading up to the stairs still had the power to surprise her. It was so opulent, so unlike her ordinary world. If not for the red path leading to the stairs pushed against the plane, she might think it simply another passenger jet. There were no markings to indicate

who the owner was—deliberately, Nico had informed her—
because it provided a certain anonymity.

They exited the Rolls and hurried up the carpet as a group
of reporters clamored from behind a line a couple hundred feet
away. Nico sent her before him, catching her around the waist
when she stumbled on the stairs and righting her.

"Careful, *cara*," he said in her ear as her heart thudded
from his nearness and the sizzling touch of his fingers through
her clothes. She made it the rest of the way without incident,
greeting the flight attendant at the door with a quick smile.

Two men sat at one of the polished mahogany tables, rising
when she and Nico entered the plush black and gold interior.
They both bowed, and one motioned to a folder on the table.

"The documents are ready, Your Highness," he said. "We
can perform the ceremony as soon as you wish."

Lily whirled to Nico. "Ceremony?"

Nico took her hand in his, squeezed, his eyes flashing a
warning. "Why wait, *cara mia?*"

"Wait?" she repeated, her brain having trouble catching up
to what, in her heart, she knew he was telling her.

"We are ready," he told the men, anchoring her to his side
with an arm wrapped around her. He looked straight into her
eyes as he said the next part, "You may marry us now."

CHAPTER FOUR

NICO WATCHED a range of emotions cross Lily's face. Shock, anger, fear—and resignation, *grazie a Dio*. She would not fight him this time.

"Why does it have to be now, like this?" she asked.

He touched her cheek, wasn't surprised when she flinched, and dropped his hand away. He'd expected her to be transformed this afternoon, but not like this. She was more beautiful than he'd thought possible. He still couldn't quite put his finger on it. Was it the smooth silkiness of her hair? The creamy velvet of her skin? Her wide, green eyes?

He didn't know, but he was having trouble remembering that he was supposed to be angry with her. He couldn't forget what she'd done to him, but now was not the time to dwell on it or to allow it to color his actions. There was plenty of time yet to deal with her treachery. And he would most certainly do so.

"A variety of reasons, Liliana," he said. "You must trust me."

She blinked. "Trust you? How do you expect me to do that?"

He grasped her arm, gently, and tugged her away from the magistrate and his assistant. Nico turned her so her view of the two men was blocked. He put his hands on her shoulders, slid them up to her face, cupped her cheeks and stroked her skin. Her breath caught, sending a warm current of need through him. *Dio,* if nothing else, he would enjoy taking her to his bed.

He might be marrying her out of honor and duty, but there were parts of it he could enjoy. *Would* enjoy.

"We must do this for Daniele," he said softly, knowing those words above all others would soothe her. He could tell her they *had* to marry now, in France, before returning to Montebianco, but he didn't think it would persuade her.

He could also tell her that his father was furious, that Antonella's father and brother were demanding retribution, and that unless they married right now, she would very probably be arrested on her return to Montebianco and thrown back into the fortress on charges of receiving stolen property and trafficking in antiquities.

He had no idea whether it was true or not—he was beginning to suspect it wasn't, though it was still quite odd that priceless art would find its way to a street vendor to be sold for a pittance. And yet nothing in her background indicated she knew the first thing about antiquities. But until they located the vendor, or caught the mastermind behind the theft, Lily was vulnerable to charges.

That was why it was now or never. If she went to prison, he would have Daniele—but his son would not have a mother. He would not marry Princess Antonella and raise his child with her; he had enough experience as the illegitimate child to know how his son would be treated by a woman who hadn't given birth to him. He would not take the chance that another woman would view his child as a threat, as Queen Tiziana had always viewed him.

Lily was the boy's mother. No matter how Nico felt about her, his son deserved a mother who cherished him.

"I want to see my son first," she said. "I want to know he's safe and well."

"He will be arriving in Montebianco very soon, *cara mia*. The plane carrying him left American airspace over five hours ago. There is no reason to wait."

She looked both elated and crushed at this news—glad she would be reunited with her baby and sad that her friend had betrayed her. Poor Lily, she'd had no idea that everyone had a price, that those closest to you could always be bought.

"It is time, Liliana."

She still looked hesitant, looked as if she would argue, so he dipped his head and touched his lips to hers—light, brief, the barest caress. And was shocked that he wanted her instantly, wanted to carry her to the back of the plane and the private bedroom there, wanted to make her his before another hour passed.

He would not, of course. When she didn't resist, he ran his tongue over the seam of her lips, testing. She opened to him, and he invaded, tangling his tongue with hers. Their strokes were light at first, teasing. And then, lightning quick, more desperate. He wasn't sure who was driving the kiss any longer, but he dug down deep and found his control, pulled back.

She looked dazed. Nico kissed her again, pressing his advantage as she leaned into him and clutched his lapels, moaning so softly that only he could hear.

When he lifted his head this time, they were both breathing a little harder. "Marry me now."

"Yes," she whispered.

Nico pulled her back to the two men before the effect of his kisses wore off and she dug in her heels again. He held her hand firmly in his, tried not to dwell on how small and cold it was. She'd not been cold when he'd known her in New Orleans. She'd been warm and innocent and vibrant. To see that gone from her now was oddly disquieting.

The magistrate said a few words, they answered ques-

tions when prompted, then signed a couple of documents—
and it was done.

"You will file these immediately, *si?*" Nico said as Lily
drifted away from his side and plopped into a seat as if she
were on autopilot.

The magistrate handed the folder to his assistant. "Of
course, Your Highness. Congratulations."

"Grazie."

The plane was airborne within minutes after the two men
left the jet. Lily hadn't moved from the black leather club
chair. She absently held the stem of a champagne glass a
flight attendant had handed her. She hadn't touched the
alcohol. Nico waved off the attendant when she came to offer
a refill. Lily turned, her expression troubled.

"How did you manage to do that? Aren't there laws that
must be followed when marrying? Didn't we need blood tests
or documents or something? We're not even French."

"Neither were they," he said. At her quizzical look, he continued. "They were from the Montebiancan embassy, *cara*.
This plane, while I am on it, is Montebiancan soil. Legally,
we were married in Montebianco, but a copy of our license
will be filed in France."

She shook her head. "I don't understand."

Nico sighed. "The marriage is recognized in France
because of a reciprocity agreement we have with them. Even
the king cannot dissolve our marriage now."

He watched as understanding clicked. She was very fast,
his wife.

"Your father disapproves, doesn't he? And you believe he
would have refused his permission?"

"Something like that, *si*. It no longer matters now. You,
Principessa Liliana, are my wife."

He thought she would say more, but she simply lifted the
glass in a mock toast. "For better or for worse." Then she

plunked it down untouched and stood, lines of strain bracketing her mouth. "I'm tired. Is there somewhere on this flying palace where I can lie down?"

"But of course," he murmured. "An attendant will show you."

Far better to send someone else with her. His blood still hummed from the kisses they'd shared. If he took her to the bedroom, it would not be to rest.

Lily was numb. She'd gone to Paris for the first time in her life, but instead of it being a wonderful memory shared with someone she loved, it was a duty she'd been expected to fulfill. She'd been married in the most romantic city on earth—yet her wedding could hardly be called romantic. She stared at the rock on her hand as they rode in silence from the airport to the Palazzo Cavelli. She, Lily Morgan from Port Pierre, Louisiana, was now a princess. She should be happy, shouldn't she?

Principessa Liliana. Princess Lily. Neither of them sounded right to her ears.

She glanced at Nico from beneath her lashes. He was so handsome, so remote, and yet he could be tender. Like when he'd kissed her. Dear God, he'd taken her breath away. She hadn't known who she was or where she was or what she was doing as his mouth slanted over hers. She'd only known hunger and a feeling of rightness that was shocking in its utter conviction. She'd been dazed and ready to do his bidding—which was certainly what he'd intended.

"Marry me now."

"Yes."

But how could he kiss her like that when only a day ago he'd been set to marry Princess Antonella and share his life with her?

Lily didn't understand, and it frustrated her. She had very little experience with men. And all of it was with this particularly exasperating specimen beside her. She had to protect herself, protect her child. She was smart enough to realize that if she didn't watch out, Nico would thoroughly confuse her. And that was dangerous for Danny most of all. He was her first priority and she must keep a clear head for him.

When they finally reached the palace, the light was waning. The chauffeur opened the door and Nico exited, turning around to hold his hand out for her.

She reminded herself he was acting a role, just as he was when he'd caught her on the stairs to the plane. It was a public facade, a show for any observers. He appeared solicitous, loving—like when he'd kissed her in front of the magistrate and his assistant. He was a very practiced seducer of women, this playboy prince.

She put her hand in his, trying to ignore the sizzle of awareness that blasted through her. As she emerged onto the cobblestone path, her attention snapped to a helicopter buzzing low overhead.

"It is the media," he said as they started to walk, her hand still caught in his. "I had hoped to keep them away for a day or two longer, but it seems as if the story has broken."

"But you said someone would call them when you bought the ring. Why is it a surprise?"

Nico's expression was stormy. "It is not the ring alone that will have brought them. Someone informed them about our trip today."

She thought of Antonella, wondered if it could have been her. But she was reluctant to say the name to Nico, unwilling to see even a hint of regret or longing in his face. Right now, she felt brittle enough that it wouldn't take much to shatter her steely facade.

"What do we do now?" The helicopter whirred closer as it made another pass.

He slipped his arm around her and guided her toward the doors that were being held open by two palace guards who snapped a salute as they approached. "We carry on as planned."

They passed between the doors and into the ornate gallery that was the main entrance. Nico stepped away from her, his arm dropping. She tried not to be disappointed, was in fact angry with herself for even considering it.

"What *is* the plan?" Lily said, her body still humming in response.

"We are married, Liliana. We will pretend to be deliriously happy with this state of affairs, *si?* You will be obedient and, while we are in public at least, you will play the role of happy wife."

Lily nearly swallowed her tongue. He'd taken everything from her in the space of hours and he wanted her to be happy? She still hadn't come to grips with the fact she would no longer be able to pursue a career, let alone that she'd suddenly become a housewife for all intents and purposes. "Excuse me? I am to be *obedient* and *happy?* What is your role in this farce?"

He looked every bit the arrogant prince in that moment. "I have had much practice at living in the public eye. I do not need instruction. You, however, do."

"So I'm to do as you say, is that it?"

"*Si,* this would be best."

"Did you not consider that I might have had a life planned before you interfered?"

He didn't look in the least sympathetic. "And how could this *life* compare with what you have gained by marrying me? You will never have to work again, Lily. Many women would kill to be in your situation."

Lily's laugh was bitter. "Oh yes, clearly they are banging down the doors. And I'd trade with any one of them in a heartbeat."

His teeth ground together before he whirled from her and strode in the direction of his apartments. She was so busy trying to keep up that she couldn't say anything else as she hurried after him, cursing the platform stilettos pinching her feet. He entered his private wing, then crashed to a stop.

Lily slammed into his broad back, cussing. "What the—?"

A child's giggle registered in her brain.

"Danny!" she cried, darting around Nico's immobile form and sweeping her little boy into her arms. "Oh my baby, my little sweetie, Mommy missed you *so* much."

She hugged him close, burying her nose in his fresh powdery scent. Until this moment, she'd feared she might never see him again. He started to squirm and she lifted her head, smiling at him so broadly her cheeks hurt. He reared his dark head back, his pale blue eyes so much like his father's as they opened wide to look at her. His little lip trembled.

"It's Mommy," Lily said, "Mommy's here. Oh how I missed you, my darling!"

Danny burst into tears.

Lily closed her eyes in relief when Danny finally drifted off to sleep. It'd scared her when he started crying, but she quickly realized she must look different to him. Plus he'd just had a long trip with a strange lady. Not that this Gisela woman seemed to have any trouble relating to him—in fact, she'd come forward quickly when Danny started to cry, and the little boy reached for her. But the last thing Lily needed was to surrender her child to a stranger and watch *her* soothe him. Not after everything else that had happened that day.

She'd ripped her hair from its confinement and mussed it up, smiling and talking to him the whole time. He'd calmed when she looked more normal to him, though he was still a bit fussy, and she'd carried him to her bedroom to lay him down for a nap. It was only midday back home, and he was accustomed to that schedule. It would take time to adjust. No one tried to stop her, and indeed she forgot all about Nico and

Gisela as she walked to the room she'd stayed in last night with Danny in her arms.

Lily's heart was near to bursting with love, but her fingers shook as she smoothed a lock of dark hair from her sleeping baby's face. She'd missed him, and she was frightened for him. For them both. Their lives would never be the same. But for now she was just relieved to see him.

She looked up as the door swung open. Nico stood there, his face clouded with a riot of emotions she didn't pretend to understand. He'd removed the jacket he'd been wearing. The contrast of the white shirt with his olive skin was stark, delicious in a way she didn't want to contemplate but couldn't stop herself from doing. Her husband was a stranger to her, and yet he was connected to her in the most intimate way possible. This child she loved so much was half his.

Half. Lily licked her lips nervously. It seemed incredible they'd come together long enough to make a baby; the man in the entry was so foreign, so unlike anyone she'd ever known. How had they gotten past those differences? How would they ever get past them again?

Nico came over to the bed, gazed down at the child sleeping amidst the pillows Lily had piled around him. Her heart pounded in her temples, her throat. They were so much alike. So very much.

"It is amazing," he said softly, a touch uncertainly. "I had thought perhaps—"

He shook his head, and Lily bit her lip. She wanted to ask what he'd thought, but wasn't brave enough to do so.

Nico reached out, and Lily instinctively grabbed his arm. "No," she said. "You'll wake him."

His tortured gaze met hers. It surprised her to see him look so vulnerable, so unsure. He was Nico Cavelli, the Crown Prince of Montebianco—and yet at the moment he looked like a man lost and alone. It made her heart ache. He dropped his hand to his side, and she felt that aching guilt all over again. Was it truly so wrong to let him touch his son? Or was she being overprotective? She didn't know, and yet instinct made her want to enclose her baby in her arms and never let anyone touch him for fear they would take him away from her.

"I have always been so careful," Nico said, still watching his child. "This was not supposed to happen."

"No," Lily whispered. "But I'm not sorry it did."

Nico's sharp gaze turned on her. "Indeed not. You have gained a kingdom out of the bargain, and more wealth than you could have dreamed possible."

Lily gritted her teeth in an effort not to scream at him. "I was talking about our son. I could care less about the rest of it."

He snorted in disbelief. "Yes, very easy for you to say when there is no question you've benefited enormously from giving birth to my heir."

Anger and hurt warred in her breast. And the desire to lash out. "I do hope you've made sure he's yours before you committed your esteemed royal self to us for life."

He looked at his son. "There is no denying this child belongs to me. But even so, I am certain of it."

A prickling sensation danced on hot feet over her skin. "How? How are you certain, Nico?"

His gaze was haughty. "No matter how strong the resemblance or how convincing the evidence, did you think I would not order a paternity test? He is mine."

Lily grabbed his arm. The muscle beneath her fingers was warm and unyielding. "You stuck a needle in my baby without telling me? How dare you!" She wasn't surprised he'd done it, now that she thought about it, nor was she surprised he could get the results lightning fast. But still, she was furious about the pain it would have caused Danny to have blood drawn. If her baby hadn't been wearing long sleeves, she'd have noticed the mark.

"Do not be a hypocrite, *cara*. He's been vaccinated, which certainly involves needles the last time I checked. It was a necessary precaution."

Lily glared at him. Her voice shook as she spoke. "Don't you *ever* do anything to my child again without permission."

"You mean *our* child, Lily." Danger saturated his words, warning her to beware. He shrugged out of her grip, turned away to look at Danny sleeping. "This is my son. He will be king someday."

And then he began speaking in Italian, shutting her out completely. Lily didn't say anything as he spoke quietly, though she trembled from the force of the emotions whipping through her. Danny was no longer solely hers, no longer her little boy to raise and love. He was a prince, a future king, an exalted being she couldn't understand from her perspective as a small-town American girl. Would he despise her someday?

She couldn't bear to think it, and she sucked in a sharp breath as Nico reached out and touched Danny's cheek. This time, she didn't try to stop him.

A moment later, he turned to her, his gaze icy. "We dine in an hour. Be ready."

Lily crossed her arms beneath her breasts. Why did she feel as if events were escaping her before she could truly understand them?

"I think I should stay with Danny. He's had a long day. He needs me."

"Gisela is qualified to look after him, I assure you. She is a very fine nanny."

"I don't want a nanny," Lily protested. "There's no need."

He shook his head, clearly pitying her. The thought made her angry. And bewildered. Why did she feel so out of sorts around him? Why did she let him intimidate her? She'd spent three evenings with him two years ago, and she'd never once felt less than his equal. Now? Oh God, now she felt as though she would never measure up, as though everything he said or did was a criticism. She was out of her depth, and she resented it. Resented him.

"You have much to learn, Lily. Princesses have many duties. A nanny is required if you are to perform them all."

Lily took a deep breath. "He needs a mother, not a nanny."

"Dinner is in an hour," Nico said. "We are dining with the king and queen. Refusal is not an option."

Lily couldn't find her voice as he walked away. At the door, he turned back. "Wear something formal. Gisela will come to look after our son."

Dinner was held in the king and queen's private apartments in a different wing of the palace. If Nico's quarters were grand, these were opulent. Lily tried not to stare wide-eyed at the priceless paintings, the frescoes and bas-reliefs, the gilding and the footmen, who looked as if they'd been plucked from another era complete with powdered wigs and silk knee pants.

Earlier, she'd thought Nico believed her incompetent because he'd sent not one, but two women to help her dress. Thank God he'd done so. She had to acknowledge that she'd have never managed alone. She was gowned in a dress as fine as anything a movie star had ever worn to a Hollywood awards ceremony, her hair was pinned into a smooth chignon, and she sported an absolute fortune in jewels. Nico had placed the diamond choker around her neck himself, and she'd put on the earrings and bracelet with shaking hands while he thankfully refrained from commenting.

And yet, in the hour since they'd been here, the queen refused to look at her and the king frowned a lot. Worse, they spoke in Italian. Or perhaps that was ideal since she didn't have to formulate responses to any questions or think up appropriate conversation.

She had no idea what they spoke about, and yet she could

see the tension lining Nico's face. Especially when Queen Tiziana said anything. His fist clenched on the table each time. She wasn't even certain he was aware of it. What must it have been like growing up with these two for parents? The thought made her shiver involuntarily.

What had she gotten herself into?

She vowed that Danny would never spend a single moment in their company without her being present. She wasn't certain if they were truly cold, or if it was simply some sort of royal reserve. Perhaps they were perfectly nice people once you got to know them—but she thoroughly doubted it. And until she knew for certain she would protect her son fiercely.

When Nico stood and informed her it was time to leave, she put her hand in his without argument and allowed him to lead her from the table. The king said something, but Nico ignored him. The king spoke again, more sharply, and Nico ground to a halt.

Slowly, he turned, spoke a few words and bowed. The king's face softened, though the queen's did not.

"Good night, my son," he said. "And goodnight, Liliana. Thank you for joining us."

Lily blinked and dropped into her best grade-school curtsy. It seemed the appropriate thing to do. "Thank you for inviting me, Your Majesty."

By the time they entered Nico's quarters, Lily had managed to work herself into a temper. Why had he forced her to endure that? It was *humiliating*. Even when she'd been working the ten to two a.m. shift at Lucky's gas station for minimum wage, she'd never been so mortified. It was as if she'd been invisible.

"What happened tonight?" she asked, an edge to her voice as she dropped her wrap on a velvet couch.

Nico's gaze was shuttered as he contemplated her. "You dined with their royal majesties, the King and Queen of Montebianco. Charming, are they not?"

She didn't think he required an answer. Indeed, he went and poured a measure of brandy into a glass, held it up in silent question. Lily shook her head. He stoppered the crystal decanter and moved to a window, his back to her, one hand in his pocket as he sipped the drink.

Oddly, she felt sorry for him. And worried for her own child. "It must have been quite different growing up in a palace," she said. "I never realized *how* different."

She turned her head to look at her surroundings, seeing them for the first time in a different light. How would a toddler ever play in a room like this? It was filled to the brim with things that could break or be stained in the blink of an eye. And with things that could injure—sharp corners, glass, small objects that could be swallowed.

In short, it was a nightmare.

"True," he said. "But I haven't always lived here. I spent the first six years of my life with my mother."

Lily blinked. "Your mother? But, I thought the queen—"

Nico laughed, but the sound was more a snort of derision. "Queen Tiziana is not my mother, *cara*. My mother died many years ago."

Lily twisted the rock on her hand, suddenly uncomfortable. Moments like this, she regretted never learning more about the man who'd fathered her child. "I'm sorry, I didn't mean—"

"It matters not," he replied. "Life is uncertain, *si?* We cannot look back with regret. It changes nothing."

She felt her anger dissipating, her curiosity about her husband growing. Clearly his life had not been one of unbroken perfection. "Where did you live before coming here? Was it very far?"

He took a seat opposite her, the brandy cradled in his palm. "Not far enough."

Lily didn't quite know what to say to that. She didn't think he meant to share so much—but perhaps he did. Did it change her opinion of him, knowing he'd lost his mother at an early age and been taken in by that icy couple sitting in their miserable grandeur on the opposite end of the palace?

She didn't want to soften toward him, didn't want to have a reason to look at him differently. He'd forced her to marry him, had bribed Carla to turn over Danny, had uprooted her life and changed it so thoroughly she could never go back. And he'd done it all without any care for her wishes.

She despised him and his autocratic ways. And yet—

"My mother had an apartment in Castello del Bianco, and a luxury villa a few miles south on the coast. It was not a bad life." He shrugged, leaned forward. "I'm sorry you had to sit through dinner with them, Liliana. My father is truly not so bad, but when the queen is near, he is more reserved. He is angry with me, but he can do nothing to change it now. He will get over it."

"I—thank you." Good grief, she certainly hadn't expected that!

He stood and set the drink on a side table. "Come, let me remove that necklace for you."

Lily's hand fluttered to her throat. Oh yes, the necklace. The one with the tricky clasp that she'd never manage on her own. He'd changed gears so quickly it threw her, but she went to him, turned and waited, her pulse thrumming so fast that he must surely see it beating in her throat.

His hands, large and smooth, settled on her bare shoulders, sent a chill skimming down the indent of her spine. Lily didn't speak, in fact didn't realize she'd been holding her breath until his fingers slid toward the nape of her neck and it rattled out of her in a shaky sigh.

"So," he said, his fingertips slipping beneath the diamond choker, stroking her skin with little motions that made her crazy, made a feeling she didn't want to examine shoot straight to the liquid center of her, "it is our wedding night, *cara*. What would you have us do first?"

"D-do?"

"*Si*, there are many things we could do." His lips touched her nape, lifted after the barest shivering caress. "Or perhaps we should go straight to bed."

CHAPTER FIVE

HE NEEDED A WOMAN. It'd been too long since he'd lost himself in the pleasures of a female body. Tonight, more than any other, he could use the oblivion a few hours of bed play would bring. He was on edge, perilously so. When he'd walked into this apartment earlier and seen his baby playing on the floor with the nanny, he'd felt as if he'd landed on a different planet. He, Nico Cavelli, had a son. *A son.*

It terrified him in the oddest way. He still didn't understand it. But for the first time since Gaetano had died, Nico wanted to walk away from his duty and his country and return to the carefree life he'd had as one of the most eligible bachelors in the world.

A life he understood. Being illegitimate, he'd never had to live his life a certain way. He hadn't been expected to marry or produce heirs. He'd lived to excess, always pulling the attention away from Gaetano. Tiziana resented him for it, but Gaetano had been grateful. His brother wasn't cut out for the spotlight, had dreaded his upcoming wedding to a woman not of his choosing.

Pain blanketed Nico. The night before his brother drove off the cliff, Nico had told him to be a man. To marry and do his duty and, for once, stop worrying about the public scrutiny.

Nico regretted that he'd not been more sympathetic, that he

hadn't listened to what Gaetano was trying to tell him. Because he knew, didn't he, what had really sent Gaetano over the edge?

No.

Nico dragged his attention back to the woman standing in front of him, her creamy skin glowing in the refracted light from the chandelier as she bent her head to allow him access to the necklace. He needed to focus on her, to shove away the pain. She'd carried his child in her body, had given birth to a son who would carry on the Cavelli name. The knowledge made him possessive.

And more. The blood of his ancestors pounded through him, urged him to storm her defenses, to conquer and pillage, to make her his and plant his seed inside her again. She was his wife now. It was right that they make a brother or a sister to join Daniele. His boy would never be lonely, not as he'd been.

Until he was brought to the palace and had Gaetano to love, he'd had no one. Before her death, his mother had used him as a pawn in her game with the queen. And though Queen Tiziana tried to separate Nico and his brother, Gaetano's love for him was mutual. They were practically inseparable until they were grown and life separated them naturally. And more than life, since Gaetano had chosen to take the final step.

Was it his fault?

"Basta," Nico muttered, turning Lily in his arms, wrapping her in his embrace and lowering his head to capture her lips almost savagely. He *would* have a few hours peace, *per Dio.*

He took her by surprise—and yet on a deep, instinctual level she'd known what was coming. Lily's head dropped back, her mouth opening beneath the onslaught of his before she could think twice about it. This kiss was like the one on the plane, but notched up by several hundred degrees.

This was what she remembered from two years ago, this all-encompassing inferno. A part of her knew she had to resist him—and yet she didn't want to. She wanted to lose herself in the heat of him, wanted to feel again all those things she'd felt before. She hadn't been with a man since that first time, hadn't *wanted* to be with anyone.

In spite of her anger at the circumstances that had bound them together as man and wife, she sensed something deeper than just a physical need in him, something that cried out for contact and closeness. After what he'd revealed to her about his childhood, she was confused by the conflicting feelings crashing through her. Had he done it on purpose to elicit her sympathy?

She didn't know, and she was on the verge of not caring why. He held her tight, his tongue stroking against hers, his mouth both gentle and fierce at once. He tasted like brandy, sweet and edgy and sharp.

Lily trembled involuntarily as he pressed her close, as the hard contours of his body fitted to the soft curves of hers. She had no doubt where he was taking them. There was something altogether bewildering about kissing this man she shared a child with. He was a prince and she was just a girl from the wrong side of town, but right now those distinctions didn't seem to matter.

She wanted him, and she wanted to push him away.

His hands slid over her back, the curve of her hips, and then he found the hidden zipper at the side of her dress. Lily dragged in a rough breath. Should she let this happen? Could she stop him?

Did she want to?

"Lily," he said against her cheek, his hot mouth skimming along her jaw, her neck. And then his lips were on hers again and she knew she was losing the battle with herself.

When her arms went around his neck, Nico knew he'd won. He would get her beneath him, get her out of his head and into his bed and place her where she belonged in his life. This crazy sense of being on a runaway train would subside and he could carry on the way he always had. Once he compartmentalized her, he would have peace again.

And yet something wasn't right. The thought niggled at him, poked at the rawness in his soul until he had to force himself to examine what was wrong. And when he did, he knew it would be a mistake to take her like this.

His history with the Palazzo Cavelli was so twisted and painful that simply being inside it affected him in ways he couldn't quite predict. After that farce of a dinner with his father and the queen, he was especially vulnerable to his bitterness. If he took his new wife now, it would be in anger.

Anger at his father, at Gaetano, at the queen—and, perhaps most of all, at Lily for deceiving him.

It was no way to begin.

He tugged her zipper back into place as he extracted himself from the kiss. She looked up at him in confusion, her pink lips lush and wet, a line forming between her brows. He put his hands around hers where they were still clasped about his neck, separated them gently and lifted them away.

"You should go to bed now, *cara.*"

When he let her go, she hugged herself, a gesture he'd noted she often did when unsettled. She looked vulnerable, confused.

He pushed his fingers through his hair, turned away from her. Away from temptation. God knew he was unsettled, too. His body throbbed with thwarted need. A long, cold shower was definitely in the cards for him tonight.

"I—"

When she didn't finish speaking, he turned to look at her. *"Si?"*

She fingered the diamond collar. "I still need your help to remove this."

"But of course," he replied, making quick work of the clasp and moving away from her as the necklace dropped.

She caught it before it fell to the floor. "Where would you like me to put these jewels?"

"Put them? They are yours, Lily. Take them to your room; stuff them under your mattress or leave them lying on the dresser. It matters not to me."

She clutched the sparkling ornament to her breast, her chest rising and falling a little faster with each breath. "I hope you aren't congratulating yourself for what just happened," she said, the color high in her cheeks.

He stifled a bitter laugh. "Hardly, *cara*."

"Because you won't catch me unaware again. Next time, I'll be ready."

Nico ignored the painful throb of his groin, the reminder he'd been so close to paradise and pushed it away. One thing he had to give her—even when she was uncertain or afraid, she barreled forward as if she knew exactly what she was doing.

"I do hope so, *bellissima*. It makes the game more fun."

Lily punched her pillow and flopped onto her side. She'd gone to bed more than two hours ago, once she'd finished her report for the *Register* and e-mailed it off, and she had yet to fall asleep. She wasn't certain what had been more humiliating—the dinner where she was ignored, or afterward when she'd practically ripped her clothes off and screamed "Take me" only to have Nico pull back inexplicably.

Inexplicably, hell. She knew why. He'd kissed her because he'd felt sorry for her after the way the king and queen treated her—or maybe it was because with her back to him, he'd been thinking of Antonella, thinking how he should be undressing *her,* kissing *her,* stripping *her* slowly and making love to his exotic princess instead of his ordinary wife.

Lily bit back a groan. Oh God, she'd really debased herself, hadn't she? She thought of the way she'd clung to him, the way she would have done anything he asked in that moment—

and felt shame suffuse her body like the glow of a hot coal. Twice today she'd been ready to do whatever he wanted simply because he'd kissed her.

She *was* pathetic. But no man had ever kissed her the way Nico did. Maybe she should have tried harder to find a boyfriend in the last year or so, find out if another man could affect her the way he did. But she'd always been so busy raising Danny and trying to make ends meet. She'd had no time for men.

And she was sorely regretting it at the moment. Maybe if her mother had tried harder to find another man, she wouldn't have been so vulnerable every time Lily's father rolled back into town and decided he wanted a place to stay. And a woman to take advantage of.

Lily turned onto her back, heard the contented gurgle of her baby in the crib nearby, and felt her exhaustion and anger melt into relief, even if only for a moment. Danny was her reason for being, her *only* reason for being. She would not lose her head over a man, and certainly not a man who didn't care for her as she deserved. Nico was smooth, treacherous. He was a playboy prince, accustomed to women falling into his bed at the mere suggestion they should do so.

He was toying with her, punishing her perhaps. She would not allow him to humiliate her again.

The next morning didn't start off so well. Lily awakened in her room alone, then panicked as she ran through the apartment trying to find where her baby had gone. In the moment she woke up, she hadn't thought of the nanny; she only knew her baby was missing. Had he crawled out of the crib somehow? He was a little dynamo, had been known to escape his crib at home a time or two as he got bigger.

She'd been ready to tear the palace apart when Nico found her in the living area calling Danny's name and on the verge of tears.

"He is not here, *cara.*"

Lily's breath froze. "Where is he? What have you done with him?"

Nico's expression grew frosty. "I've not kidnapped him, Liliana. He is fine."

For once, Lily felt chastened. But only slightly. "I want to see him."

"You cannot." He checked his watch, then speared her with the full force of his stare. "We are retiring to my private *palazzo* for a few days. I have sent Gisela ahead with Daniele. They will meet us there. You must get dressed."

Though Lily was furious with him for making a decision about Danny without consulting her, it did no good to rail at him. He merely shrugged it off and told her to hurry.

Now, she sat beside him in his silver Maserati and watched the miles fly by as they snaked toward their new abode. Montebianco was far more beautiful than she'd realized. At one point, they drove through a lush, almost tropical forest before emerging onto the coastal road. Around every corner, cliffs jutted out to sea, their white faces stark and beautiful. Below, the turquoise water lapped their bases.

In fact, the farther Nico drove, the less traffic they encountered and the fewer homes, except for those perched on the cliffs overlooking the Med. It was all so exotic, so exciting. She, Lily Morgan—no, Lily *Cavelli*—was zipping along the Mediterranean coast with a prince. Who would have ever thought it?

The sun was strong and bright, and Lily was thankful she'd gotten new sunglasses that wrapped around the corners of her eyes to minimize the light. She'd been uncertain how to dress, but she'd finally chosen espresso capri pants with a cream top and a pair of low-heeled sandals. Her French-manicured toes looked very elegant, she thought. Nico hadn't commented on her attire, so she supposed what she'd chosen was appropriate.

"How far is it?" she finally asked after they'd been on the road for nearly an hour.

Nico glanced at her. "So you do remember how to talk."

Lily shifted in her seat to look at him. "I was waiting until I could speak without the urge to shout at you."

His mouth lifted in a grin that sent her heart skittering. "It took a long while, yes?"

"I'm sure the urge will return quite soon," she replied. "This conversation may be brief."

He laughed, a warm rich sound that she'd not heard since they'd sat together at a restaurant in the French Quarter two years ago. She'd forgotten how much she enjoyed the sound. She'd been captivated with him then, and his easy laugh had certainly been part of the charm.

"We are nearly there," he said. "You've wasted the entire trip pouting."

"I was not pouting."

"Indeed you were. I am quite accustomed to women's moods, *cara*. I recognize pouting when I see it."

Lily chewed her lip. Mention of his experience with women did nothing to enhance *her* mood. She chose to ignore it and move on. "What will we do in this new place that we could not have done in Castello del Bianco?"

Nico's hands flexed on the wheel. "We will have some peace from the curiosity seekers, for one. And far fewer people to deal with. No king and queen nearby. We can play on the beach, take walks, swim. It is like your American vacations, yes?"

Vacations weren't something she'd ever had time for, but she understood what he meant. She latched onto something he'd said. "What do you mean by curiosity seekers?"

He seemed to consider for a moment. "You cannot imagine our hasty marriage has not garnered attention."

"No, of course not."

He glanced at her again. "You are new to this, Lily, but you must realize that the media will go to extraordinary lengths to pry into our lives, to find stories to tell, and some of those stories may embarrass or anger us. It is something you learn to live with."

"Don't you fight when the stories are wrong?" The *Port Pierre Register* was small, and yet they always printed corrections when someone disputed an article.

He shrugged. "It is almost never worth the effort."

"No one bothered you in New Orleans. I would have certainly remembered if you'd gotten media attention."

"*Si,* this is true. But I was in the city anonymously, and my brother was still the Crown Prince. The American media are not so interested in European royalty, yes?"

Lily tucked a lock of hair behind her ear as she watched him. "You have a brother?"

His jaw tightened as he concentrated on the road. For a moment, she thought he might not answer. "*Had* a brother, *cara mia.* He is dead."

"Oh." Impulsively, she reached out and touched his arm. "I'm sorry."

"*Grazie.* He died two months ago and I miss him every day."

Lily swallowed a lump in her throat as she turned away. She'd been so focused on Nico as a tyrant and a playboy that she hadn't imagined him to have a softer side, a side that felt deep emotion and experienced pain. Of course she knew he must, but she'd not expected he would let her see into his life like this. Not so soon anyway.

Just then, they rounded the final turn and a sprawling complex appeared before them. It was sleek, modern, not at all what she'd expected. "I thought you said we were going to a palace!"

"It is a palace—but it is *my* palace. I had it built a few years ago, and I consider it home." He pressed a button in the car and the black iron gates swung open to admit them. Moments later, he pulled into a sleek garage beneath the house and shut off the engine.

Inside, the house was nothing like the ornate confection of his apartments in the Palazzo Cavelli. The furniture was sleek, modern. Soft leather couches, hardwood floors, plush Oriental rugs, and modern art. It was very masculine—and yet, it was beautiful in its restraint.

Nico looked at her. "We will probably spend a lot of time here, *cara*. If you wish to change something, this is possible."

She shook her head slowly. "No, I'm not sure I would change a thing. I like it."

"Nevertheless, if you should change your mind." He tossed his keys onto a table behind the sofa. "Now, if you wish to see Daniele's room, follow me."

The house was large, but not as big as the palace, so when they came to her baby's room she wasn't quite prepared for the sight that greeted her. Toys filled every corner of the room, giant stuffed giraffes, pandas, a bear—Lily's hand went to her mouth as she took it all in. The furniture was grand—a plush couch, an entertainment center with a flat-screen television, a chair—but there was no crib, no dressers. Perhaps there hadn't been time. He'd only learned he had a son two days ago.

Nico grinned at her. "It is a suite, Lily. Here." He took her hand, led her through the room, into a palatial bathroom, and out the other side to another grand room—only this one had a crib, dressers, a changing table and a wall of bookshelves filled with children's books. Gisela sat in a rocker, but she popped up and curtsied when she walked in. For the first time, Lily realized how young the girl was. She was barely twenty, Lily would bet. Far too young to know about babies. She made a mental note to speak with Nico further about this nanny idea.

"Mamamamamamamama!" Danny cried, wobbling toward her as fast as he could on his little legs.

Lily's heart filled. She dropped to her knees and held her arms wide as her baby ran headlong into them.

"Mama," he said contentedly as she stood and hugged him tight.

"Who's my little Dannykins? Who's mama's baby? Is this mama's baby?"

Danny giggled in delight as she pulled his shirt up and blew a raspberry on his belly. She laughed, then glanced at Nico. His expression was not at all what she expected. A mixture of pain and anger played across his handsome face. She turned away, cradled Danny against her as her heart picked up speed.

"Mama," Danny said again, then began babbling something unintelligible. He stretched his arms out, trying to get down, and she set him on the floor again. He promptly toddled back to the little truck he'd been playing with on the soft carpet.

Nico watched Danny play, his nostrils flaring, his jaw tightening. He flexed his fingers at his side, though she didn't think he was aware of it. It was as if he wanted to move, wanted to touch Danny—but couldn't bring himself to do it.

And it hit her that he must feel like a stranger in this little triangle. He was the one left out, the one looking in.

"He's learning new words all the time," Lily said softly, her mind reeling with conflicting thoughts. Danny was his son, and they were strangers. Could she bring herself to help him? She frowned, torn between the desire to keep Danny to herself, to protect him, and the knowledge that she was being selfish, that Nico was Danny's father and her son deserved the best father possible. If Nico remained the outsider, how would that benefit Danny?

Lily swallowed her trepidation. "If you went and played with him," she said, "it would help him get to know you."

Beside her, Nico stiffened. His face, when she dared to look, was a blank mask. But his eyes—

Oh God, if his eyes were flames, she would surely be burned to a crisp in them right this second.

"It will take time," she offered, trying to make him understand. "But you have to—"

Nico turned and left the room.

CHAPTER SIX

LILY WENT AFTER HIM, but Nico knew the house much better than she did and he was gone before she could catch him. She stood in the empty living room, uncertain whether to keep looking for him or to return to Danny.

Why had Nico left so abruptly? She'd been trying to help him, trying to make him understand it would take time to get to know his son. The pain on his face had twisted her heart, pricked her with guilt. It was her fault he was a stranger to Danny. In that moment, she hadn't liked herself very much and she'd wanted to make it right.

Unable to find him, she eventually went back to Danny's room, sent Gisela away and played with her baby until he crashed. As she tucked him into his crib, a fat tear dropped onto the back of her hand. She scrubbed it away, then dashed her hands beneath her eyes to get rid of the rest of them.

What was her problem? She'd tried to help, but Nico refused her advice.

She needed to move around, needed to burn off some of her restless energy. She found Gisela on the couch in the other room and asked her to please keep an eye on Danny while he slept. Then she wandered the big house, poking into rooms and stepping onto myriad terraces that all had fabulous views of the sea. She hoped she might find Nico, might explain to him that he needed to spend time with Danny, that it would all be well if he would do so. But he wasn't in the house.

She found the clothes he'd bought for her in a closet the size of her apartment back home. Another closet, as masculine as hers was feminine, adjoined it, and she knew she'd probably stumbled into the master suite. Beyond the closets, a bathroom the size of a small city had floor-to-ceiling windows that looked out at the ocean, and a giant spa tub sunk into the floor in front of them.

Unbelievably, there was a butler's pantry attached, complete with a refrigerator and wine rack. Perfect, she supposed, for entertaining guests in the tub. Female guests, no doubt.

Princess Antonella?

Lily shoved the thought aside with a mental growl. She hesitated at the bedroom door, then slid it open on silent rollers and stepped inside. It was a large room with a king-size bed that dominated one wall. Again, floor-to-ceiling windows looked out on a view as spectacular as any she'd ever seen. She crossed to the terrace doors, but stopped when her attention was caught by a trio of framed photos on a table beside a club chair.

In the first, two boys, close in age, stood with their arms around each other, smiling. The next was of a young man, caught in a moment of exuberance, laughing at the camera—Nico's brother, she guessed. The third was a formal portrait of Nico as a child; it must have been shortly after he'd come to the palace. He looked so solemn. Unhappy. He wore a uniform much like the one he'd had on the other night, though without the medals, sword or sash.

Lily picked up the photo, studied it. The resemblance to Danny, even now, was remarkable. She wondered why the picture was important to Nico, why he displayed it when the boy in the frame looked so unhappy. Didn't most people surround themselves with photos that evoked pleasant feelings?

"It reminds me of who I am."

Lily whirled, clutching the frame to her chest. "Oh God, you scared me."

Clad in head-to-toe black, he looked as dark and devilish as any demon. It took her a moment to realize he was dressed in motorcycle leathers. For some reason, her heart rate jumped.

He rode a motorcycle? He raced the hairpin curves they'd driven on the way out here? Challenged the sheer drops that plunged to the sea? How could he be so irresponsible? What would they do if something happened to him?

He came to stand beside her, the scents of warm leather, wind and, yes, even oil permeating her senses. Her nipples tingled in response, shocking her. Her boyfriend in Louisiana, before she'd ever met Nico, had worked on a farm. He'd often smelled of grease and outdoors, and she'd never once found that sexy.

But Nico, a gorgeous, wealthy prince—

The contrast aroused her for some reason. Pathetic.

His shoulder bumped against her as he pointed at the picture of the two boys. "Gaetano is on the left."

"He's not as tall as you," she said stupidly, only half paying attention. Threads of fire spread through her at his nearness, currents of sweet need thickening her veins. What was wrong with her? Why could she not control this feeling when he was around?

"*Si*, and he was older by three years. Very interesting, yes?" He didn't wait for an answer. "The other is a few years later. Gaetano was laughing at something, I don't remember what. We went to Australia that summer, and I'd never seen him freer. It was quite extraordinary, but then you would have had to know my brother to understand."

"Maybe he didn't like being the Crown Prince," she ventured. Who would, as unhappy a place as the Palazzo Cavelli seemed to be?

Nico nodded slowly, surprising her. "Yes, I believe it was that. And more. He never told me exactly."

Lily thought of her mother, how she'd never understood the choices the older woman made. The way she lived her life for one man in particular, then fell apart during the periods he was gone. Maybe it wasn't the same thing, but at least Lily understood what it was to love someone and not understand them or be able to penetrate the armor they cloaked themselves with.

"What happened to him?" she asked softly.

Nico took the frame she still held, gazed at the child in the photo. "It was suicide, *cara*."

Shock and sorrow crashed into her. She'd known a girl in high school who took her own life. The blow was too much for her parents to weather; they'd divorced not quite a year later, and the mother left town. The girl's brother had withdrawn, too, finally quitting school and spending time in jail. All their lives had been irrevocably changed by that one act.

How had Nico's brother's death affected him? The king and queen?

"I'm very sorry," she said. "No one should lose a family member like that."

It seemed such an inadequate thing to say, but it was all she could do. He kept his gaze focused on the photo. "No, no one should," he said.

She wanted to ask him more about his brother, but she was afraid to do so. She was, in fact, amazed he was even talking to her after the way he'd looked at her earlier. She wanted to reach out and hug him, but instead she changed the subject.

"How old were you in that picture?"

"Six. My mother had died three days before."

He couldn't miss her indrawn breath. There'd been so

much pain in his life. It broke her heart to think of it, to think she'd contributed even a fraction to his sorrow.

Leather creaked as he shifted toward her. "It was not so bad after a while. I adapted."

She felt her eyes filling. "But you were a boy. You should have had more time."

"Life does not always cooperate, *si?* I lost my mother, but I gained a brother."

A brother he'd lost, as well. "No one should only get one or the other."

"No, this is true."

"Was it very bad? Being raised in the palace, I mean?"

"I have nothing else to compare it to."

She couldn't imagine the queen being very kind to a motherless boy, especially one whose presence reminded her that her husband had gone outside their marriage vows. "You must have missed her. Your mother."

"I hardly remember her now, *cara.* She was always busy—and then one day she was gone."

Lily swallowed the hard lump in her throat. *No child should be that lonely.* She stood beside him, unmoving, feeling his presence so strongly that his every breath felt as if it were her own. She could not have moved away if her life depended on it.

But he could. He set the photo down and stepped away. In the next instant, the oily *zrrittt* of a zipper filled the silence before his jacket landed on a chair. He stood before her in a tight white T-shirt that clung to sweat-dampened muscles. His hair, she realized, was also damp and hugged his head in a mess of runaway tendrils that she ached to touch.

The leather pants were tight, well-worn in patches from gripping his legs around the motorcycle. He also wore heavy black boots with buckles that cinched over the pants, and she found her breath catching in her chest.

It wasn't fair. He threw her off balance looking like that, like every girl's bad boy dream. She could see him roaring up to a smoky nightclub, riding off into the night with a woman wrapped around him—a woman who knew a night of sinful pleasure awaited her.

Lily wanted to be that woman. She wanted to peel the shirt from his chest and lick her way down—

Oh God.

"Need something, Lily?" he asked softly.

Her pulse quickened. "No, I—" She pulled in a deep breath. "Of course not. Why do you ask?"

"Perhaps I can give you what you need," he said. "You have only to ask."

"I'm—" *Breathe, Lily.* "No, it's nothing. I was just thinking about something. I'm sorry, what were you saying?"

"It is not important," he said, watching her. "I'd much rather talk about what *you* were thinking."

"I—I better go see if Danny's awake," she replied, shivers chasing over her body. How did he do this to her? How could he look at her with such hatred earlier and then flirt with her now?

Because he was an expert, that's why, a Don Juan who'd seduced hundreds of women. She could not forget who she was dealing with. He didn't care about her. He was merely reacting to the vibes she was giving off.

Stop it now, before you do something stupid.

Nico closed the distance between them. "What's the matter, Liliana? Afraid to admit what we both know?"

She tilted her head back, meeting those piercing eyes, the depths that were awash in humor and something more. Desire?

"I'm not afraid of you," she said.

His smile was instant. Devilish.

Delicious.

"Did I say you were?" He reached out, twirled a lock of

her hair around a tanned finger. It was only hair, yet she trembled as if he were stroking her skin. "It's inevitable, Lily. We *will* end up in bed together. Quite probably sooner than you think. There is no need to fight it."

She had to struggle to speak normally. "I'm not fighting anything. You're delusional."

"Am I?" His fingers slipped to her collarbone, stroked their way up her neck to her jaw. He grinned when he passed over the thrumming beat of her pulse. "Perhaps we should test this theory…."

Lily marshaled what shreds of willpower she had left and jerked away from him. "There's nothing to test, Nico."

He didn't try to touch her again, but his mouth was still crooked in that knowing grin. His voice was a sensual purr. "Run, Lily. Run far and fast before you find yourself sprawled naked on my bed. Because if we begin this, I will not stop until it's finished."

Her entire body shook with fear. No, not fear. *Desire. Need. Want.*

In another minute, she'd be the one shoving him backward onto the bed, the one tearing at his shirt and slipping her hands into his pants—

Lily ran, his mocking laughter following her down the hall.

Nico slid beneath the shower spray, the cool water a welcome relief from the heat of his wild ride along the coast. No, it was more than that. He needed the cold water to calm his raging desire for his wife. *His wife.*

Only a day later and he still felt a mixture of amazement and bewilderment that he had a wife, much less one that twisted him up inside unlike anything he'd ever experienced. It was simply her proximity, the fact she was desirable and that he hadn't had a woman recently—not to mention the way she'd looked at him a few minutes ago.

As if she'd spent a week in the desert and he was the first glass of water she'd seen in all that time.

He'd been more than willing to quench her thirst. He still had a hard-on, damn her. He let his soapy hand slide over it, groaned. He could relieve himself, certainly, but it wasn't the same. He twisted the shower dial to cold and resisted the urge to shout as the needles of icy water pierced his skin.

He closed his eyes, leaned his forehead against the tile and willed his raging libido to subside. For now anyway.

How could he want her like this when he'd watched her with his son earlier and had it driven home how much he'd missed in his boy's life thus far? Danny—for so she always called him—said *mama.* He walked. He knew who his mother was and ignored the man standing beside her.

Ignored his *father.*

She'd urged Nico to go play with the boy, but he'd felt like his heart was on the outside, like if he did so she would see how uncertain he was, how much it hurt to be a stranger to his child. He didn't know anything about children, not really. He'd spent minutes with them, not hours. He, who was in supreme control in every other instance of his life, had no idea what to do with his son—and it bothered him.

Instead of going to his son, he'd fled. *Dio,* like the worst kind of coward. But he'd felt too much in that moment and he hadn't quite known how to handle it. A long ride on his Ducati with the wind slipping past and the purr of the motor beneath him was exactly what he'd needed to clear his mind.

When he thought back to that moment when his baby ran to Lily, every feeling he'd ever had of not belonging, of being the outcast, crashed through him once more. Remembering those feelings helped him not want Lily so much.

But he still wanted her. And he knew what he needed to do. He would not creep around his own house, avoiding his wife and remaining a stranger to his son. No, he would learn how to be a father to his boy—and he would bed his wife.

Very soon, she would beg for his touch. She'd nearly done so just now. If there was one thing on this earth he knew how to do—and do well—it was seduce a woman. Though he could command her to share his bed, the idea was nearly laughable. Prince Nico Cavelli did not ever need to order women to get naked for him.

He would not start now, and certainly not with the woman he'd married.

Lily was feeling quite cranky when she woke and dressed the next morning. She'd spent the night in a state of flux—one minute she was cold, the next hot and throwing off the covers. Unfortunately, all the times she woke up in a sweat coincided with short, intense dreams about a certain prince in motorcycle leathers.

She hadn't dreamed of sex in a long time, but she'd more than made up for it in the span of one night. She'd had shadowy impressions of skin against skin, of his lips against hers, of his hot velvet length sliding inside her, filling her so deliciously that she thought she might die from the pleasure of it.

She could almost believe those things had really happened if she hadn't awakened alone each time, panting and aching with desire. No matter how delectable her dreams, she had to resist the temptation to give herself to him. Because down that path lay ruin and pain. She wasn't naive enough to think she could manage a lifetime with him without being intimate— they were married and he would want more children, as did she—but there had to be a point at which she could isolate that most vulnerable part of herself and keep it locked away.

It would simply take time to find it, but she would do so. For her sake, and for Danny's. Until then, she would have to be careful.

When she emerged from her dressing room, she first went to Danny's room. He wasn't there, so she continued toward the kitchen. This time, she wasn't panicking that Danny'd been spirited away.

Lily heard voices and smelled food as she approached the kitchen, but the sight that greeted her when she stepped inside the large, sunny space was not one she could have ever expected. Nico stood at the stove, a pan in one hand, a spatula in the other. He smiled when he saw her, and her heart tripped.

"Ah, so you have decided to grace us with your presence after all."

"It's only eight-thirty."

"Yes, but we have been up since six."

She looked beyond him to where Danny played in a corner with a set of building blocks. When he saw her, he launched to his feet and toddled toward her, babbling happily. She caught him in her arms and covered his face in kisses while he laughed.

When she looked at Nico, he'd turned his attention back to the pan. "What are you making?"

He glanced up. "Eggs. For you."

Lily's eyebrows climbed toward her hairline. "For me?" she practically squeaked.

"Si." He grinned at her. "Do not look so frightened, *cara mia.* I am capable of cooking quite a few things, eggs being one of them."

"Why would a prince need to cook?" She'd imagined him with a personal chef and a staff of waiters, had seen it in action in the palace in fact. But she'd never imagined him cooking. And never for her. That was certainly not something that happened in any of the fairy tales she'd ever read. What an unexpected man her prince was turning out to be.

"Princes need to know many things," he said, moving the spatula around the pan. "Besides, the queen considered it edifying to have me learn tasks she thought menial."

Lily frowned. "Did your brother learn them, too?"

"He did, but only because he defied her to be with me." He shrugged. "Let us not talk of this anymore, hmm?"

Danny started to struggle and she set him down. He immediately went back to his toys. "You watched Danny all morning?"

She sensed the sudden tension in the set of Nico's shoulders, and it troubled her. Why was he afraid to spend time with his son? Did he think she would disapprove? It bothered her to realize that only twenty-four hours ago, she would have. And, while a part of her was still jealous at the idea of Danny needing anyone but her, she wanted what was best for her child.

A father—a happy, involved father—was best for them all.

"Gisela fed and dressed him, and we have been playing for the past hour while she uses the gym."

"Gym?"

Nico grinned at her again. "You are full of questions this morning, *Mi Principessa*. Food will cure that, perhaps. But yes, there is a gym in the house. Very good for keeping one's figure."

She imagined him pumping iron and thought her heart would stop, especially when her brain insisted on clothing him in leather pants and a damp T-shirt. He indicated a bar stool at the large center island. Then he set a plate in front of her, and she dug in with her fork while he poured coffee.

"Wow, it's good," she said, and he laughed.

"You did not believe I could do it, did you?"

Lily couldn't hide a smile. "No, I really didn't. Who would risk telling a prince his eggs taste like burned cardboard? I thought perhaps no one ever told you the truth before."

She stabbed her fork in again, took another bite of the perfectly scrambled eggs. They were creamy, silky and tasted like butter. How much time had he spent in a kitchen anyway? Lily decided she disliked the queen even more. "It really is delicious."

"I would have done this for you two years ago," he said,

jolting her with the memory of that morning, "but we had no kitchen in our room."

She took a hasty sip of coffee, hoped she could blame the rush of heat to her face on the hot liquid. This was too intimate, sitting here with him as if they were a happy couple, and she felt too exposed. She didn't want to talk with him about that night, not now. Perhaps if she moved on to the most obvious contradiction, he would leave it alone. "It must have been quite an experience for you, spending the night in a cheap hotel like that one."

His eyes gleamed wickedly. "I don't remember the room, *cara*. It had a bed. The rest is unimportant."

"You left before I woke." She knew her voice held a note of accusation, but she couldn't seem to prevent it. She'd been disappointed that morning to find him gone—but he'd left her a scribbled message, and she knew it was only a matter of hours before they would meet again.

Except he'd never shown up. And she'd cried for two days when she realized how foolish she'd been. She'd given herself to a man who'd used her for his pleasure and abandoned her.

How familiar was that?

He placed a hand on hers where it rested on the marble counter. "I did not want to go, but duty called, as I have said before. Unfortunately, it also called me back to Montebianco when I found out the true extent of the problem."

"What happened?"

She *wanted* to understand. The feelings she'd experienced had been so new, so amazing and tender, and she'd wanted to keep them for far longer than she'd been allowed. That had been her first real heartbreak. Because a part of her had fallen hard for the man she'd chosen to give herself to, and the truth of how wrong she'd been about him had been devastating.

His thumb traced a path on the back of her hand, sending

spirals of sensation rolling through her in waves. "It was the first time my brother attempted suicide, Liliana."

His sadness lanced into her. She'd been so focused on herself and her feelings about that night that she hadn't considered something terrible might have happened. And now she felt that aching guilt again. It was almost as if the universe had conspired to keep them apart.

Silly. Even he had been there that night, it wouldn't have lasted between them. He was a prince, for pity's sake. She was no one.

"I'm really sorry, Nico. I can't imagine how hard it must have been for you and your family to go through that with a person you loved."

He caught her chin in his fingers, forced her to look him in the eye. "And it must have been difficult for you when I did not return, yes? I would have been there had it been possible."

Perhaps he would have. But she refused to dwell on it. That naive girl was gone, buried under the weight of harsh reality and motherhood. She pulled free of his grip. "We can't change the past."

"Yes, but—" He looked down, his brows drawing together. "*Si,* little one?"

Lily dropped her fork and pushed herself up in her seat, leaning as far as she could over the island. Danny stood beside Nico, clutching his pant leg with one hand. The other arm was stretched up, his little hand opening and closing. A sharp pain pierced Lily's heart—but was it joy or fear?

"He wants you to pick him up," she said softly, biting her lip hard to keep her silly tears from spilling.

Nico looked at her for a split second, a mixture of terror and confusion on his handsome face. She could have laughed if her heart weren't breaking. "It's okay, Nico. Pick him up. He'll want down again in a minute."

Miraculously, he bent over and scooped Danny into his

arms. And then he looked at her as if he feared he'd need more instruction. Danny, for his part, looked thrilled at the new heights he'd reached. Nico was indeed tall, and Danny seemed to delight in it.

Finally, he put his arms around Nico's neck and burbled a string of unintelligible words.

"What did he say?"

Lily shrugged and tried not to laugh. "I wish I knew."

"I thought women were supposed to understand baby talk."

"I know when he wants something, but sometimes it's not so clear. He likes the sound of his voice, I think."

Danny touched Nico's nose, then touched his own. *"Naso,"* Nico said. "Nose."

Danny laughed. The sound coaxed an answering smile from Nico while Lily could only stare at them both in wonder. Two dark heads so close together, smooth olive skin—Nico's was darker, of course—and eyes that could be a mirror to the other when they both turned to look at her.

Nico frowned. "Why do you cry, Liliana?"

"What? Oh." She swiped the tears away guiltily. "It's nothing."

"Ma-ma."

Lily smiled. "Yes, baby boy?"

He stretched his little arms toward her. She looked at Nico hesitantly, but he was already leaning forward, letting Danny reach for her. A second later, she had her baby in her arms. She tickled him, blew raspberries on his belly while he laughed uproariously, then kissed his little face until he protested. Another minute and he was down, his attention caught by the blocks once more.

"He is amazing," Nico said with that sort of singular pride that all parents had in their babies.

Lily felt a bubble of joy lifting toward the surface of her

soul. "Oh yes," she said solemnly, "the most amazing baby in the world."

Nico looked at her, his mouth crooking into a grin. A second later, they were both laughing.

The next few days were some of the most idyllic of his life. Nico spent time with Lily and their son without any expectations. He continued his slow seduction of Lily's mind and body, not rushing the process in the least. He was in fact enjoying it. He touched her as much as possible, brushing up against her as he passed, reaching across her to pick something up, his arm skimming her breast if he could manage it.

It was driving him crazy, touching her without *touching* her. He wanted to strip her, explore her with his hands and mouth, wanted to do all the things he'd realized were impossible due to her inexperience the first time. He wanted to spend days learning her body, wanted to know what drove her crazy and what made her come unglued in his arms.

He was driving himself crazy, but more importantly he was driving *her* crazy. When they made love for the second time, it would be well worth the wait.

He was also, gradually, becoming more comfortable with his son. He no longer felt stirrings of panic when Danny wanted to be picked up, no longer worried he would drop him or hold him wrong. In fact, it was almost ridiculously easy to make the child happy. Why had he not realized this before? Tickle him, make faces, talk silly—and the little guy was fascinated. So, Nico realized, was Lily.

Still, he didn't play with their son because it made her happy. He played with him because it made Danny happy. And Nico.

For the first time since Gaetano had died, he felt content. He took his little family to the beach, took them for drives and hunted down obscure restaurants where the owners were discreet and they could enjoy themselves like anyone else. He'd had the reporters who'd camped at the gates to the palazzo run off, and he'd been pleased they hadn't returned. Only one helicopter had invaded his privacy, but a single phone call and it was gone, as well.

After yet another day at the beach with Lily and Danny, Nico strode into his office to find a letter from his father waiting. Nico ripped into the envelope—the man was too old-fashioned to use e-mail—and scanned its contents.

As expected, King Paolo of Monteverde remained an unhappy man. Paolo was widely reputed to be violent, though Nico didn't think the king would go so far as to initiate hostilities between the countries simply because his daughter had been jilted.

He dropped into a chair, unmindful of the sand clinging to his body, and propped his forehead on his hands. The truth was that Montebianco could suffer if the trade issues didn't get worked out. His country depended on olive oil, textiles and raw ore from Monteverde. They could procure the items elsewhere, certainly, but at what cost? How many jobs would be lost? How many households would suffer a reduction in their income?

Nico had counted on Monteverde's dependence on Montebiancan wines, leather goods and produce to even the balance and make King Paolo see reason.

But the king was more stubborn than he'd anticipated.

Madonna diavola.

As much as he wanted to stay out here with his head buried in the sand, it was time to return to the Palazzo Cavelli. Montebianco's people needed to know their prince was concerned about their welfare, that his pleasure took a backseat to their future. He could not let them down.

The day before Gaetano had died, he'd said, "*You* should

have been Crown Prince, Nico. You're stronger, more capable. Montebianco needs a man like you."

Nico had told him not to be so ridiculous, told him he was a fine prince and would be a good king. Gaetano had only smiled.

But later that day, they'd argued.

"I don't want to get married, Nico," Gaetano had said for what seemed the hundredth time.

Nico, tired and frustrated with his brother's reluctance to do his duty when he'd always been so privileged, had lashed out. "Sometimes you have to do what you do not want, Gaetano. It's your duty as Crown Prince, as our future king."

Gaetano had looked at him with such sadness. "But I *can't* be a husband to her."

"Dio," Nico had said, pushing shaky fingers through his hair. "All you need to do is get her pregnant, ensure the succession."

"You don't understand, Nico. I can't. She's, she's—"

Nico had feared what was coming, had said firmly and without sympathy, "You can. You *must.*"

Gaetano had looked away, swallowed. To this day, Nico regretted not letting his brother say what had been on his mind. *I can't because she's a woman, Nico.*

Why had he been afraid to hear it? Why, when he'd always known? Why hadn't he simply hugged his brother and told him he loved him, no matter what?

He'd never gotten the chance to say those words. Early the next morning, Gaetano drove off the cliff.

Nico would give anything—*anything*—to bring him back again. Since he couldn't, he would do the only thing he knew how. He would honor Gaetano's memory by being the kind of Crown Prince his brother believed he would be.

He would do his duty, no matter the personal cost.

CHAPTER SEVEN

LILY'S HEART CLIMBED into her throat and took up residence there. "You want to do what?"

Nico came into the room, swinging a helmet from one hand. "Come with me, Liliana. It will be fun."

His expression didn't exactly look fun loving. No, if anything she'd say those were lines of strain around his eyes. "I—I've never ridden a motorcycle. I don't know how."

"You have only to hold on to me." He caught her around the waist with one broad hand, pulled her toward his leather-clad body. "You can do that, *si?*"

If she fainted from the light-headedness he induced in her with his mere presence, would she get out of the ride? It was a thought. But there was something in his eyes, something that told her she didn't want him to go alone.

"I'm not sure it's safe."

Nothing about Nico was safe. Over the last few days, he'd managed to somehow make her like him the way she had in New Orleans. In spite of the way they'd begun this time, her heart was bound tighter each time she saw him with Danny. Whether he tried to teach their baby Italian, talked nonsense to him or made him giggle, Lily felt herself melting a little more with every moment they spent together.

Having a baby changed people. Had it changed Nico? Was

he enjoying fatherhood? Was Danny as important to him as he was to her? The evidence said yes, but she'd learned not to trust herself so easily. Her father had often made her mother happy for varying lengths of time before he broke her heart yet again. It was a lesson Lily needed to remember.

Especially now, when he looked like sin wrapped up and tied with a bow.

"We will go slowly, I promise."

She motioned at his delicious fantasy of a body. Oh that formfitting leather! She hadn't been able to get it out of her mind since the first time he'd worn it. "I don't have the appropriate attire."

"Jeans, boots and a jacket will do for where we are going."

She blinked. "Where would that be?"

His smile was genuine, and it sent her pulse into overdrive. "It's a surprise."

Fifteen minutes later, Lily found herself climbing onto the back of a wicked-looking motorcycle and cinching a helmet into place. She wrapped her arms around him while the engine hummed and the smell of leather, rubber and motor oil filled her nostrils. The bike was sleek—red and silver—and purred like a kitten. Until he revved it.

Lily clutched him tighter as they roared up the drive. The gates opened and he shot between them. A news van sat around the corner from the entrance, and it launched forward as they passed.

"Maledizone," Nico said, the sound coming clearly through the helmet mike. There were a few more words in Italian—which she decided were not in the least polite—and then he said, "Hold on, *cara.*"

"Nico, please," she said, her heart thrumming as she thought of her sweet baby back at the house, of the last few days of bliss—oh God, *why* had she agreed to this? "I don't like going so fast!"

"Trust me," he replied. "A few moments, we will lose them. I will not hurt you, Lily."

She didn't reply, simply tightened her arms around him and laid her head against his back. The motorcycle was designed in such a way that she sat higher than he did, and when he leaned over the bars, she had to lie against him or let go. She chose to flatten herself against him.

The bike roared at incredible speeds down the coastal road. "We are approaching a turn. Lean the way I do, *si?*"

As if she could do anything different. He braked only a hair, then arrowed into the corner, dipping deep to the left, laying the bike nearly flat—and then they were out the other side as if they'd been fired from a gun. Her breath stuck in her chest.

She dared to turn her head as much as possible against the wind and blurring landscape. Behind them, the van was nowhere to be seen.

"I think you lost them!"

"I can hear you, there is no need to shout."

"Sorry."

"Another few minutes, and we'll get off the road."

Lily held tight to his torso, finally breathing again when the motorcycle slowed. He made a turn onto a path that led downhill. It was a dirt trail, wide, and lined with brush. They rode on it for several minutes before he turned again and they emerged onto a remote beach.

He took the motorcycle down to the water's edge and drove along the packed sand there. They went slow enough that Lily was able to sit up and gaze out at the cresting waves. A dark band of clouds had moved in, blocking the sun. The day had gone from bright to gray in the space of a few minutes.

"Will it rain?" she asked.

Nico looked up. "Possibly."

He didn't seem too concerned, so she didn't say anything else about it. A few minutes later, he slowed even more, then came to a stop beside a huge ragged limestone rock that sat like an island in a sea of sand.

"Take my hand and climb down," he said. "Be sure to watch out for the pipes. They are very hot."

Lily did as he instructed, removing the helmet while Nico swung a leg over and stood on the sand beside her. He unsnapped his helmet and tugged it off. "That was fun, yes?"

"Um, not all of it," Lily said. "It was a little fast."

"Sometimes fast is best," Nico said, his mouth lifting in that wicked grin that always sent her heart into overdrive. He appeared more at ease now than he had when they'd started. She wasn't sure what had changed for him, but she was glad for it.

He set his helmet on the seat, placed hers there, as well, then took her hand and led her toward an outcropping of rocks a few feet away.

"Where are we going?" she asked again.

"We're almost there."

She had no idea what he wanted to show her. Another rock? More sand? She'd thought he'd already taken her to some of the more beautiful spots on this coast. They rounded the cliff face and Lily jolted to a stop.

Nico turned back to look at her. He seemed oddly solemn. "It is extraordinary, isn't it?"

Lily could only nod. The cliff face bowed inward at this point, creating a half-round bowl that held the skeleton of a wooden ship. The vessel lay on its side, the wood darkened through years of enduring the elements. The remnants of a tattered flag flapped in the strong breeze coming from the direction of the ocean.

"Is it a pirate ship?" she asked, and then felt silly for doing so. She'd been watching too many Hollywood blockbusters.

"No. In fact, it's not all that old. It is a replica of the days when Montebianco's wealth came from command of the shipping lanes. But it sank in strong seas during a regatta many years ago and washed up here."

"Why wasn't it moved to a museum?"

He shrugged. "Not enough interest, I suppose." He walked toward the ship, and she followed, her imagination spinning out a tale. Though he wore leather, she could easily picture him in breeches, standing on the deck and commanding his men to sail into battle. And though the ship was a replica, it made her think of the history of this country and the long line of kings her husband must descend from.

The long line of kings her son descended from.

And suddenly she felt so out of her depth that it frightened her. What was she doing here? Why had a prince—a future king—married *her?* What happened when he realized she was completely unsuitable?

He would take Danny from her and send her back to America, that's what.

No.

He would not do such a thing. He couldn't. He'd lost his own mother, hadn't he? That had to count for something.

He bent over and grabbed a rock, then hopped up onto one of the thick logs at the base of the ship and hurled it. Lily stopped and watched him, her memories of the last few days tumbling together with her fears. He seemed preoccupied as he put his hands on either side of a gap in the hull and peered inside. Eventually, he pushed away and turned back to her.

His expression changed in a heartbeat.

"Cavolo!" He jumped down and ran toward her. "We must get under cover," he said, grabbing her arm and spinning her back the way they'd come. That's when she saw what had alarmed him.

Black clouds hung lower in the sky than before, and the wind picked up speed, whipping her hair across her eyes. She could taste the salt on her tongue from the cool air, and she scraped her hair away so she could see. A funnel cloud danced along the water, moving toward the beach.

"Is that a tornado?" Good God, they had tornadoes here? She'd thought those were a nightmare she'd left behind in Louisiana.

His voice was grim. "It is a water spout. Probably won't come ashore, but the rain will be quite hard for a while." They reached the motorcycle and he tossed a helmet to her. "Don't put it on," he said when she started to do just that. "We don't have time to get away."

"What are we going to do, stand here beside this rock and hope for the best?"

"There is a cave nearby. We'll wait inside for the worst to pass." His smile belied the seriousness of the situation. "Don't worry, *cara,* the sun will be shining again in half an hour."

He wheeled the bike toward the cliff, skirted along for a few feet, then slipped between an opening in the white rock. Lily followed, not sure what she'd find inside. A tiny, dank space where she couldn't see two feet in front of her face? The idea did not make her happy.

But no, the cave opened into a large area with a roof that soared thirty feet or more. Light filtered in from gaps in the rock much higher up the face. The walls glittered with what looked like tiny crystals.

"It was a sea cave once," Nico said, parking the motor-cycle and turning to face her. "Millennia ago."

Fine, powdery sand covered the floor, punctuated here and there by rocks. He went over to a ledge of smooth rock against one wall and sat down. "I used to come here with my brother," he said, as if in answer to her unspoken question about how he knew where to find it. "It was very far from the family palazzo, and forbidden—but we did so anyway."

Lily imagined the two boys in the picture, laughing and running and knowing they were doing something wrong but unwilling to stop. "Did you come often?"

He leaned back against the rock, hands clasped casually on

his knees. "Not often, no. It was very far, and difficult to get to. We found the ship one summer, and we tried to come as often as possible. As you can imagine, a wreck would have much fascination for young boys."

Outside, the rain began to beat against the rock. The wind whipped inside the cave, stirring up the sand. The storm had moved very fast. She imagined them caught in it, shuddered. Thankfully he'd known where to take them or they would be huddling in the wind and rain right this moment.

"Come," Nico said, holding out an arm. She went and sat beside him, reveled in the warmth of his body as he tucked her in against him. Maybe she should have said no, but she didn't want to. Not this time.

Nico's chin rested on her head, and she found herself burrowing closer, her arm going around his waist. It seemed natural, inevitable. If only they could stay like this forever.

"Gaetano died here," he said softly, and she jerked back, her eyes searching his face. The pain in his eyes was raw— and yet controlled.

"Nico, I—"

"Shh," he said, pressing a finger to her lips. A thrill of sensation shot through her. "It's okay, *cara mia*. He made his choice."

"What happened?" she said when he took his finger away.

"He drove his car off a cliff nearby."

Lily shuddered. How awful for them all. "Why did you want to bring me here if it makes you sad?"

He tilted her chin up, his eyes capturing hers for long moments. But then they closed, and he leaned back, away from her. "I sometimes think he's waiting here. I know he is not, but it gives me comfort to think so."

Lily couldn't help herself—she cupped his smooth jaw in her palm, spread her fingers along the fine, strong bones of his face. He felt closer to his brother in this place, and he'd brought her with him. It touched her more than she could say.

"I don't think that's wrong," she said softly. "It happened so recently, you're still growing accustomed to it."

He pressed his hand over one of hers, then dipped down and touched her lips with his own. Gently, lightly—so lightly that she was the one to lean forward, the one to demand more.

But he did not give it to her. "There is something about you, Liliana," he said, his breath hot against her skin. "I don't know what it is."

"Perhaps you just don't know me very well," she replied, her heart thrumming as their breaths mingled. It was so intimate, so thrilling. She *wanted* him to kiss her again, as he had the night of their wedding. He hadn't attempted it in days now, and she was a little too uncertain of herself to kiss him first. "I'm a mystery."

He leaned away from her, and she bit back a protest. Not at all the effect she'd been aiming for. She wanted to howl in frustration.

"Then tell me something."

She gaped at him, a hot achy feeling settling in the pit of her stomach. "Isn't it usually the woman who wants to talk first?"

Nico threw back his head and laughed. Lily tried not to join him, but she couldn't help herself. It felt good. A week ago, she'd have never thought she could share a light moment with him—and yet, in the space of the last few days, she'd seen a side to him she'd only hoped existed.

Was that the real Nico? Or was she dreaming of something that wasn't truly there?

"Indulge me, Liliana. Tell me something about yourself."

"I don't know what to say," she replied, her eyes downcast as she felt suddenly shy. What could she tell him that wasn't mortifying? He was a prince, completely unaccustomed to the sort of life she would have led in Louisiana.

"Surely there is something."

"I'm an only child."

"I know that." When she looked up, he was smiling gently. "I know the facts, *cara*. I don't know how you feel about them."

All the facts? That was a rather frightening prospect. Lily twisted her fingers into the fabric of her jacket. How could she reveal her deepest longings and hurts to him? "I've never had the luxury of dwelling too much on the past."

"Were you lonely without siblings?"

"Sometimes. But I had friends. I had Carla," she said, frowning.

"Do not blame her, Lily," he said, going to the heart of what she was thinking. "Very few people can resist the lure of such money, especially when they do not have it."

"I don't *blame* her," Lily said. "How could she say no? You wouldn't have let her anyway." She couldn't blame Carla, though it still hurt. Would she have done the same thing if their positions were reversed? She liked to think she wouldn't, but how could anyone know what they would do until faced with the choice?

"No," he said very solemnly. "I would not."

"And has the price been worth it?" A coil of heat threaded through her veins. He'd bought her and her son as though they were chattel, had put her friend in an impossible position. It still had the power to anger her when she considered it. Their lives were forever altered now.

"I believe so, yes," he replied. He caught her hand and brought it to his mouth, sucked the tip of her finger. "I'm not sorry, Lily, because our son is worth any price to me."

Am I?

Lily shivered, but she could not ask the question. "He is the best thing that ever happened to me."

"And the most frightening, no?"

"It wasn't easy, if that's what you're asking. But I wouldn't trade it."

"I know you would not." He dropped her hand, shifted

away from her on the stone ledge. "You had no right to keep him from me for so long."

Lily swallowed the lump in her throat. She'd thought she was doing the right thing for her baby, but now she realized she'd hurt the man who'd fathered him with her silence. They still had a long way to go, but he seemed to genuinely adore his son. "No, I should have contacted you."

His gaze was sharp. "Do you mean this?"

"Yes." She glanced away. "I—I was afraid you might take him away from me."

His eyes burned into her. "We still have much to learn about each other, it seems."

Feeling somewhat awkward in the silence that followed, Lily leaned back to look up at the soaring ceiling; outside, the rain pounded down. "We get storms like this back home, but they can be much worse. I was terrified of thunder when I was little."

"But not now?"

Lily shook her head. "No. I had to stop being afraid. I was often alone in the house, and I'd have gone crazy otherwise."

It was hard staying frightened when you had to learn to take care of yourself because your mother was off in some bar or another. Storms ceased to be significant.

"But you were afraid for a while, yes?"

Lily sucked in a breath. "I learned to deal with it. It was that or go around jumping at every little sound and hiding under the covers whenever it rained."

"That seems reasonable," he said gently. "Though it couldn't have been easy."

Lily shrugged. "Nobody ever said life was easy."

Nico's gaze was thoughtful. "I'm learning what it is about you, I think," he said, his voice barely reaching her as the rain picked up outside. "You are strong, Liliana. Brave. I find this very compelling."

"I—"

He swooped in and cut her off with a kiss, his mouth claiming hers hotly. It was shocking, but Lily had no wish to argue about it: she opened to him. Their tongues met, sucking and stroking—pulling her deeper under the tidal wave of desire cresting inside her body.

This. This was what she wanted, this spark, this beautiful passion. All of it, hers.

"*Dio,* I want you," he said against her mouth.

"Yes."

The knowledge sent a thrill through her. He wanted *her.* Not Antonella, but her.

Strangely, she wasn't scared. She'd had sex with him once—had only had sex *once* in her life. And, oh God, she was burning up with the desire to do it again. It'd been pretty good that first time, though mysterious and somewhat frightening, too. But now?

Oh, now…

She knew what to do, knew what to expect. Lily ached with the need for release, felt as if she would die if she didn't reach that culmination. To hell with her fears. Right now, she wanted her prince.

She put her arms around his neck, pressed in closer. He was warm and big, his body sizzling against hers. One of his hands worked the buttons on her shirt, spreading it open as he moved downward. The air wasn't all that cool, but against her heated skin, it felt like an arctic breeze. Lily shivered, not from the chill, but from anticipation.

When Nico had her shirt open, he spread the material wide, his lips blazing a trail down her neck, over her collarbone—

Lily gasped as his mouth grazed the soft mound of her breast. "It's a front clasp," she managed, and Nico chuckled before releasing the bra and freeing her breasts from the lacy cups. He shaped them, pressed them together, and she leaned back on her hands, thrusting her chest up, toward his seeking mouth.

She wanted him inside her. Her body ached with it. More than anything, she wanted to feel the heat of him, the hard length of him, his naked skin against hers as they moved together. There had been pain the last time, just a little, but she knew there would be none now—in spite of the fact she hadn't had sex again since that first time, she was more than ready for him.

When his lips closed over one tight peak, she thought she would come simply from the exquisite sensation.

"Oh, Nico," she gasped.

He growled low in his throat, a sound of possession and male satisfaction. The vibrations shuddered through her, gathered in the center of her feminine core and threatened to shatter her senses. How could she be on the edge so quickly?

He laved each nipple with his tongue, dragged his teeth across the aching points with just enough pressure to make her back arch toward him.

She couldn't allow it, couldn't be the only one about to explode with the feelings and sensations of all he was doing. Lily reached for the snap to his pants, smiling to herself as his breath rattled in on a sharp hiss.

The sound emboldened her, and she tugged his zipper down enough to get her hand inside. He was hard, his penis thick and hot beneath her hand. He growled at her again as she wrapped her fingers around him.

"Lily, *Dio*."

And then he dragged her into his lap, kissed her hard. She stroked him, tentatively at first, then more boldly as he shuddered beneath her touch.

Finally, he tore his mouth away. Swore. "Stop, Liliana."

"But you like it," she said, shocked at how sensual her voice sounded.

He grasped her wrist, pulled her hand away from his pants. "It is not a question of like, but a question of control. Keep doing that, and we'll be finished before we begin. I want you too much for play."

"Then we need to begin."

He closed his eyes, swallowed hard. "*Madonna diavola*, had I known you would be so eager, I would have taken you to bed and skipped this ride."

Heat crept up Lily's neck to her cheeks. "Had you kissed me first, maybe we'd still be there instead of here."

Nico kissed her knuckles, laughing brokenly, while she tugged her shirt back into place with her free hand, suddenly self-conscious and confused at his hesitation.

"No," he said, catching her fingers and opening her shirt again.

"Nico, for heaven's sake, what's the point if all you're going to do is talk?"

"Your eagerness is most gratifying, *cara mia*. A man likes to know he is wanted."

As if he'd ever had a problem with *that*. "So does a woman," she shot back.

"Oh, I want you," he said as he stood and started shrugging out of his jacket. The dark T-shirt he wore molded to his muscular torso, and Lily dragged in a deep, sustaining breath that smelled of salt and sea, hoping it would steady her erratic heartbeat. The man ought to come with a warning label that proclaimed one word loud and clear: *Danger!*

"Then what do you plan to do about it?"

His lip curled in a wicked smile. "As many things as I can get away with."

CHAPTER EIGHT

SHE INTRIGUED HIM as no woman had ever done. Nico allowed himself a small frown as he slipped out of his leather jacket. No, that wasn't quite right. He was certain he'd been fascinated with other women before Lily. *Hadn't he?*

But it'd been a long time since he'd wanted one so badly he was ready to spill himself like an eager teenager. Even now, looking at her, he had to keep a tight rein on his need. She sat on the ledge, her hair mussed, her lips swollen from his kisses. Her shirt and jacket gapped open, exposing her soft breasts, the high-tipped points of her nipples and petal pink of her areolas. Quite simply, he wanted to devour her.

He was torn between taking her here in this place and waiting until he had a soft bed to lay her down in. But his baser nature didn't want to wait. And apparently, neither did hers.

"Come here," he said, tugging her up and against him. He tossed his jacket on the smooth ledge where she'd been sitting, then dropped his mouth to her exposed collarbone, followed the line of one shoulder as he pushed her shirt down her arms. He wondered if she would protest, but she went for his waistband again. He hissed when she closed her fist around him. She'd certainly learned a thing or two in the last couple of years.

The thought of another man making love to her, while his son lay in a crib in another room, repulsed him. *Infuriated him.* She should have been his. All this time, she should have been *his*.

He wrapped a hand in her glorious hair and tugged her head back, exposing her neck to his questing mouth. A moment later, he let her go and unfastened her pants. He couldn't wait another second to see her, to touch her womanly softness.

"Nico—" She gasped as he shoved the material down, dropping to his knees in front of her. She was trapped by her pants and boots, but he was free to do whatever he liked. A state of affairs he intended to take full advantage of. His cock strained against the confining leather, the ache driving him almost to distraction. He wanted to thrust into her, *now.*

But he would deny himself until he'd given her this.

Her buttocks were round and smooth in his hands as he pressed a kiss to her belly. He intended to go slowly, to drive her as insane as she was making him, but the satiny feel of her, her womanly scent, the heat and lushness—he couldn't wait.

Nico licked a path down her abdomen, sliding into her femininity, finding the little point of her pleasure. He spread her with his fingers, ran the flat of his tongue over her clitoris, varying the pressure.

Her fingers wound in his hair as she threw her head back, little panting sounds of delight bursting from her. She was eager, wet, her body humming with the tension he wound tighter and tighter. He knew not to let her go over yet, backed away each time he sensed she was close. He wanted to drag it out, wanted to give her so much pleasure she would never desire another lover.

He slipped a finger inside her tight passage—and her knees buckled as she cried out. Her body clutched at him greedily as she shuddered and shuddered.

Dio, she'd reached her peak.

Just like that.

The wonder of it staggered him. He held her up when she

would have dropped, stood and lifted her onto the ledge when the tremors subsided. She was so wild and beautiful in her abandon, leaning back on her arms, her breasts thrust into the air. Another moment and he would free himself, would thrust into her and—

Her eyes were closed, tears slipping down her cheeks. He stilled in the act of unsnapping the leathers. He ached to touch her again, to take her over the edge and show her how beautiful it could be between them. But for the first time ever, he stared at a woman and found himself uncertain.

Had he hurt her? But no, she'd gotten pleasure; he knew she had. Maybe he'd gone too fast, driven her relentlessly to the point of surrender and now she regretted it.

Or was it something deeper? Had he pushed her too far when he'd asked her to tell him about herself? Had he forced her to reveal too much of her soul?

Yes, he knew many things about her—but he felt as if he knew nothing. Facts on an investigator's report weren't the same as whispered confidences.

And then it hit him. The idea was so ridiculous he almost rejected it out of hand. But, *per Dio,* he wanted her to love him. His entire body stilled as he absorbed the idea, examined it from all angles. He *wanted* her to love him. He wanted *one* person in this world to look at him with the kind of loving adoration his brother had. It was the only feeling of belonging he'd ever had, and he missed it. Perhaps that's why he'd brought her here today: it was an effort to merge the two very different halves of his life.

Was he that transparent, that desperate?

Nico drew in a breath, closed his eyes. He needed time to think. The rain had stopped, and the sharp smell of the sea filled his nostrils. He would take her home, give her time to recover, give them both time to regroup. He couldn't push her now, not like this. She deserved better.

"Liliana," he said, reaching for her shirt and jacket and laying them across her. His penis throbbed in protest at what he was about to do. "Put these on and we will go."

Her eyes glistened as she sat up. "W-why? You haven't—"

"Shh." He dropped beside her, her taste still on his lips, his body screaming for release. "The storm is over, we need to go before we are missed."

A tear spilled over her cheek and he caught it before she could scrub it away. "I don't understand," she whispered.

"It is best this way, *cara.*" The hurt shining in her eyes bewildered him. Wasn't he doing the right thing? He shoved away from her and refastened his pants. Behind him, he could hear her dressing.

A moment later, she was passing him, grabbing her helmet off the motorcycle and waiting for him to push it out to the beach. He picked up his jacket and crossed to the bike.

"Why do you always back away?" she demanded. The other side of passion was anger—and she looked like a pint-sized Amazon, eyes flashing, cheeks flushed, hands on hips.

Always? He'd stopped himself twice, both times against his will. And he was damn sure paying for it the way his body ached. "Now is not the right time," he told her. "It's not you."

She dragged in a laugh that ended brokenly. "'It's not you, it's me.' I've heard that before, Nico. Usually it happens when some high school boy wants to break up with you because he's heard that the girl down the road is an easy lay."

Nico kicked the stand from the Ducati and blinked at her. She was angry with him when he was being considerate of her? When he wasn't falling on her like an animal? Frustration crashed into him. "What the hell is an 'easy lay'?"

Her chin quivered. "A moment ago, I'd have said me."

It took him a second to process the English idiom, but then he understood. "Lily—"

"Don't say anything to me right now, Nico. It won't help."

He considered it as he watched her fight with herself, realized she was right. They'd already come too far down this path to turn back. There was too much hurt and anger to make it right at the moment. He wheeled the bike from the cave, Lily on his heels.

They rode back to the house in silence, humiliation a drumbeat in her veins. Nico had proven his mastery over her, had made her desperate for him, and then walked away as if she were as easy to dismiss as an annoying fly. He gave her an orgasm, certainly, but how embarrassing was it to fall apart like that under his expert attention and then have him zip his pants and tell her they had to go, as if he'd done something as mundane as tuned up the motorcycle?

And why, *why* had she said that to him about high school boyfriends? God, how pitiful and revealing was that? Before she'd gone to New Orleans and met Nico, her longtime boyfriend—the one she thought she might marry someday—had broken up with her because she wouldn't sleep with him. She'd believed that if she gave away her virginity, she'd somehow become like her mother. So she'd guarded it fiercely—until Jason broke up with her and she'd met Nico a few short months later.

When they arrived back at the house, Lily went immediately to the shower and tried to scrub the feel of his lips and tongue from her body.

It didn't work. Nothing worked. She only wanted more.

Heaven help her.

She couldn't figure him out. One minute he was hot and vibrant and on the edge of control; the next he was cool and collected and so in control she wanted to scream. It wasn't fair, not when she couldn't seem to find her balance around him no matter how hard she tried. Just when she thought she had it figured out, he did something to shake her up.

And whoa, he'd certainly shaken her up in that cave. She couldn't erase the image of him kneeling before her, his mouth on her body, waves of sheer bliss thundering through her like the surf outside.

But what happened next wasn't at all what she'd anticipated. She'd expected him to join her on the ledge, to slide into her and ease the incredible ache she'd still felt.

Except he'd lied—or he enjoyed manipulating her. She wasn't sure which. But the truth was that he didn't want her as much as he'd claimed he did. He wanted Antonella, perhaps—or one of his sleek mistresses. He did not want a low-born American girl who was more mutt than pedigree. In fact, she wouldn't be surprised if he'd left the palazzo again and went to one of his many female admirers for comfort.

Though wouldn't a womanizer take what was offered to him? Why would he go that far and no further? God, she didn't know! She didn't understand him at all.

Much later, when she couldn't sleep, Lily decided to go to Danny's room and check on him. Gisela was close by, of course, but Lily just wanted to sit in the dark and listen to her baby breathe. If she were with her baby, she'd find her center of balance again.

She'd wanted to keep Danny in the room with her, as she'd done since he'd been born, but she had to admit it was time he had his own room. Though it was hard to let go even that much, she didn't want him growing up frightened to be alone in the night.

Lily slipped into her robe and made her way down the hall. She padded into the outer suite on silent feet, then crept into Danny's room—

And drew up short. An ocher night-light burned against one wall, casting a soft glow on the room—illuminating the man who lay on the chaise with his son on his chest. Against her will, Lily's heart knotted.

Man and boy slept soundly. Even in sleep, Nico had a protective arm over Danny, anchoring him in place. The sight brought her both joy and pain—joy that they had each other, and pain that her baby now had someone else besides her.

She hesitated on the edge of the threshold, uncertain whether to go or stay—would Nico's hold on Danny eventually relax? Would her baby fall to the floor? Or did her husband have the situation well in hand?

Lily bit her lip, warring with herself so intently that she didn't notice Nico's eyes flutter open. When she looked at his handsome face again, he was staring back at her. Her heart turned over in her chest. He was a beautiful sight, masculine and strong—and yet tender enough to hold a sleeping baby.

Wasn't that what every woman wanted?

Carefully, he shifted Danny and sat up. She rushed forward to help him, but he shook his head and she crashed to a halt, her fingers twitching with the urge to assist. He managed to rise and lay Danny back into the crib. Her little boy curled into a ball, his arms wrapped around the blue plush dinosaur he'd fallen in love with. His old teddy bear sat in one corner of the bed if he needed it.

Lily joined Nico beside the crib, reassuring herself that Danny was indeed asleep. Then, the two of them left the room. When they'd gone a short distance, Lily asked, "Was he awake when you went in?"

"I heard him crying." Nico ran a hand through his hair. "It took a long time for him to sleep."

Lily's heart was in her throat. "Danny was crying? Why didn't you call me? Where was Gisela?"

"Gisela is feeling unwell, *cara*. I told her to go back to bed."

"You should have called me."

"Why? What could you have done differently?"

Nothing probably. Lily bit her lip. "I'm his mother," she said defensively.

"I am aware of this."

Oh God. When he used humor on her, she wanted to melt into a sticky puddle. She crossed her arms, trying to shore up her defenses. She absolutely would *not* think of how amazing his mouth felt on the most sensitive part of her.

"Perhaps I should go back, stay with him—"

"No."

Lily gaped at him. "What do you mean no? You can't order me around like I'm the hired help. I'm his *mother,* and if I want to spend the night watching over my son, I will."

He took a step closer, his large form crowding her in the darkened hall. She refused to step backward, though her pulse kicked up. He smelled like citrus and spice, with the faintest hint of an ocean-scented breeze. To her dismay, she wanted to lick him like a lollipop.

"There is no need, Lily. He's asleep. It's simply an excuse to get away from me."

"That's not true." Except it was.

"You still want me and you don't like it."

She lifted her chin. "You really are full of yourself, aren't you?"

"I know when a woman is—how do you say—*turned on.* You, Liliana, are very much so."

"You're kidding yourself if you think so," she said coolly. "You had your chance, Nico. You turned it down."

He tilted his head, let his gaze slide down her body and back up again. The perusal was slow, thorough, and her blood pressure spiked at the heated look in his eyes. But she'd experienced that look before, hadn't she? And it hadn't mattered one damn bit.

She stared back at him with all the iciness she could muster.

His smile was wolfish. "Very good, *cara.* You will make a fine princess yet."

"Don't mock me, Nico."

"I would not dream of it, *Mi Principessa.*"

For a moment she thought—or was it hoped…feared?—he was about to kiss her anyway.

His expression changed, seemed troubled for a moment. But then it passed. "I forgot to mention we are returning to Castello del Bianco in the morning. You must be ready by eight."

Just like that, he'd changed direction again. Fury burned through her. "I'm not doing this," she vowed fiercely. "I'm not living the rest of my life taking orders and jumping to your tune. Is this how you would have treated Antonella? How you would have treated *anyone* but me?"

"Keep your voice down before you wake Daniele."

How dare he insinuate she didn't care about her baby's welfare! Lily shoved him as hard as she could. Which didn't amount to much since he only moved back a single step. The next second he'd wrapped his hands around her wrists. Then he pushed her against the wall, trapping her arms above her head.

His head dipped toward her. Lily turned away, pressed her cheek to the wall. Rejected him the way he'd rejected her earlier.

He nibbled her earlobe. Lily's eyes closed as a current of need rocketed through her, settled in her core. She bit back the moan that tried to escape, but not before he heard a fraction of it she was sure.

"*Dio,* you are fiery. And I've been too careful with you," he said. "I erred on the side of caution when I should have done no such thing." He transferred her wrists to one hand, then used the other to slide beneath her robe and cup her breast. "Perhaps I should take you to bed and keep you beneath me for the rest of the night."

"You talk a fine game," she managed, her heart drumming as her nipple rose to his touch, "but we both know you won't do it. You don't seem to have any staying power."

She'd thought he would be angry at her insult, but a laugh rumbled in his chest. "Now that," he said, "is where you are wrong."

"Then why do you keep stopping before you begin? Maybe you have a *premature* issue or something and you don't want me to know you can't keep it up long enough to—"

His bark of laughter startled her. The next instant, she was in his arms and he was striding down the hall. He kicked his way into the nearest room. She realized it was his as he set her down and ripped his dark T-shirt over his head.

As he advanced on her, naked chest gleaming in the soft lamplight, she scrambled backward, torn between resisting and helping. A dark line of hair arrowed down toward faded jeans, which rested just below his hip bones and showcased the hard muscles of his abdomen. He was a spoiled prince, and yet he looked like a demigod, all bronze and delicious with a sculpted body, tousled hair and bedroom eyes.

Sexy.

That was the word that popped into her head as he reached for her. So incredibly sexy.

"You're not going to force me," she declared. "You wouldn't do such a thing—"

"I might," he said, unknotting the belt of her robe, "but I doubt it's necessary."

"No matter what you think, you aren't irresistible, Nico."

The robe fell from her shoulders; he grabbed the hem of her favorite sleep shirt after taking a second to grin at the cartoon cat on the front. His expression grew serious. Hot. "I might have believed you had I not tasted your desire earlier. Are you wet for me now, too, Lily?"

Before she could formulate an answer, the shirt disappeared and he was pushing her backward onto the buttery-soft leather couch in the sitting area. He followed her down, his naked chest against her skin, the rigid bulge in his jeans riding against her silk panties.

And she realized she hadn't yet tried to resist. Lily closed her eyes, swallowed hard against her doubts and insecurities. "Stop, I don't want this."

She didn't sound very convincing.

"You are a poor liar, Liliana." His head dropped, and then his teeth were scraping her jaw, his big hands spanning her hips, lifting her against his erection.

Lily bit back a moan. What was wrong with her? How could she let him do this to her? She'd trusted him earlier, trusted that he wanted her the way she wanted him, and he'd made a fool of her.

He would do so again if she let him. He took pleasure in tormenting her like this.

"No," she gasped as his mouth closed around one aroused nipple. His fingers slipped beneath her panties, found the sensitive heart of her desire.

"You *are* hot for me, Lily."

She gasped as he stroked her. "Nico, no."

He stilled, lifted his head, his eyes searching hers. "Tell me to stop, right now, and I will do so. But if you don't say the word, Lily—" he softly squeezed her clitoris, eliciting the most delicious sensation "—if you don't tell me to leave this instant, there will be no turning back, *capisci?* You *will* be mine."

Her lungs stopped working as she gazed up into his handsome face. He was heart-stoppingly beautiful, and he was about to make love to her. Or was he?

"I want you to stop," she blurted. Because if she didn't say it, if she didn't make him cease this sweet torture, he would humiliate her once more.

Nico looked at her in disbelief. And then he swore violently. But his hand slid up, out of her panties—

Until she caught his wrist. She wasn't even aware she'd done so until he looked at where she'd grabbed him.

"What's it going to be, *Principessa?*"

Oh God, he'd given her the choice. He'd lobbed the ball

into her court and she was messing it up badly. Her heart pounded, her vision tunneling in on the man above her. She could see nothing but him, nothing but his piercing eyes and sculpted features. But she couldn't let him go.

"Tell me you want me," he commanded.

"I—I can't."

He reversed the progress of his hand, slipped between her folds again. Her eyes closed as he found her.

"So wet, Lily. So ready for me. Why would you want to deny us this?"

"You denied us first—"

"I thought you needed more time, that I'd pushed you too fast. Clearly, I was wrong."

One finger entered her, then another. Slowly at first, then faster, he mimicked the motion of what he would do with his body.

"Nico—"

He made a sound low in his throat. "Do you like this?"

"Yesss."

"Do you want more?"

"I—yes."

"Good, because I am through waiting, *tesoro mio*."

She moaned in protest when he lifted away from her, but he unsnapped his jeans, shoving them down just enough to free himself. Lily could only stare as his penis sprang free. He was more than ready for her. And, oh my God, she was a lucky, lucky woman.

Nico lowered himself onto her again, hooking his fingers into her wispy panties and shoving them aside. She'd forgotten all about them while she'd devoured his body with her eyes.

Suddenly, she knew this was it. He was done with prelimi-naries, done with the give-and-take dance that had gotten them to this point. There was no turning back now. Fear gripped her—and anticipation.

He lifted her hips with one broad hand beneath her bottom and drove into her.

Lily cried out from the shock of it. This was what she'd wanted from him earlier, this incredible pressure and tension, the sweet aching beauty of male possession. But not just any male—*this* male, this gorgeous, amazing man.

"Lily, *sei dolce come il miele,*" he groaned.

She had no idea what he'd said, but it sounded beautiful.

"You feel so good." His eyes were closed, his head tilted back. "I want to stay like this…."

Lily wrapped her legs around him, lifted herself until she could catch him around the neck and pull him down to her. She had to taste him. "Kiss me," she begged. "Please kiss me, Nico."

His mouth fused to hers, hot and wet, his tongue plunging into the moist recesses of her mouth to tangle with her own. He moved his hips, sliding away from her while she tried to hold him tight.

And then he plunged forward again and her scalp tingled. *Everything* tingled. Every last nerve ending, every last cell. Her entire body was alive with the sensations of what he did to her.

What they did to each other. Because Lily was not passive, not this time. She might not have had sex again until this moment, but she'd had a baby and she was no longer naive. Her pleasure was as much her responsibility as it was his.

She ran her hands down his sides, cupped his buttocks as she lifted her hips to him. Her body was ready for him, and yet she knew she would be somewhat tender when it was over. And she didn't care. She pushed up into each long stroke, meeting him at the top, the pressure more exquisite each time.

"Lily," he groaned. "What you do to me, ah *Dio*…"

"Don't stop, Nico. Please don't…" She squeezed her eyes shut. "I can't…can't last…it's been so long…."

He growled something in Italian, something hot and

dark—and then he let go of his control. Soon they were both beyond restraint, slamming into each other urgently.

As the tempo increased, he buried his face against her neck, his breathing as ragged as her own. She could feel it coming, hovering on the edge of her senses, the culmination of an orgasm that was so much more complete than the one she'd had earlier. That had been blissful, shocking—but this, oh, *this*.

Her breath caught as the first tendrils of it uncoiled inside her. Nico seemed to sense it and angled her pelvis higher so the pressure changed as he stroked into her.

And Lily exploded into a million bright lights. A moment later, Nico followed, his hips grinding into her as he came, a broken groan spilling from his lips. A groan that sounded like her name.

But she couldn't be sure because she was still trying to gather the pieces of herself back together.

Long minutes later, he pushed away from her. She mourned the loss of him, but welcomed the cool air where it flowed over her sweat-dampened body. She lay with her eyes closed, one hand flung over her face, trying to process everything that had just happened.

In two years, she'd not felt even the slightest stirring of desire for any man. Nico was the one who'd filled her dreams, who'd starred in her fantasies, the one who'd fathered her precious child. But Danny was the product, not the reason, of what she'd felt for him that night two years ago.

Was it love? Fear wrapped around her like ice. She could *not* be in love with him. It was far too soon, and she didn't know him well enough. But her heart didn't seem to care.

"*Dio,* Lily, you feel amazing." He lowered himself and ran his tongue across her belly, spread his fingers over her abdomen. "These marks—are they from the pregnancy?"

She tilted her head up. He traced a fine, silvery stretch mark. It was so fine she was surprised he'd noticed. But then, it wasn't as if she'd been naked for anyone since having Danny. How would she know what a man might notice?

"Yes."

He bent to trace it with his tongue. "I'm sorry I did not get to see you carrying my child."

The comment made tears press against the back of her eyes. Until his fingers fanned over her possessively, stroking her sensitized skin. His dark head moved up her torso, and then his mouth fastened on a distended nipple. Lily clutched him to her, the sweet tension in her body nearly unbearable.

She hadn't recovered from the last orgasm and already she wanted him again. He made her feel special, cherished. Hot and achy.

He suckled her other nipple, advanced and covered her mouth, his tongue dipping inside to tease and torment.

"We should move to the bed," he murmured between long, deep kisses. By the time they made it, she'd lost her panties and he'd lost his jeans—and then he was inside her again....

And Lily knew she was the one who was lost.

CHAPTER NINE

NICO COULDN'T breathe properly. Every lungful of air was filled with the sweet scent of the woman beside him—she smelled like flowers and spring rain with a hint of cinnamon; she smelled like the Lily he remembered. He gently traced the line of the sheet where it lay above the swell of her breasts. He ached with the need to lose himself in her once more, but he knew he should not demand it of her. Not again tonight.

She lay with her head to one side, her eyes closed, her chest rising and falling evenly. They'd both fallen asleep after the second time, but now he was awake—wide-awake—and wondering what he should do.

If she'd been one of his mistresses, he'd have dressed and left her apartment. Not that he never spent the night with a woman—he often did—but just as often he felt the need to return to his own home and enjoy his solitude. Tonight he wanted no such thing.

"Nico," she breathed.

"Yes, *tesoro mio?*"

"I should check on Danny again—"

"I went a little while ago. He is sound asleep. As you should be." He threaded his fingers between hers, kissed her knuckles.

"You're not."

"I do not need much sleep."

"Maybe our son gets it from you then," she said, yawning. She turned into him and he wrapped his arms around her, pressed her naked body against him. Why had he waited so long to take her to his bed? He dipped his head, touched his lips to her shoulder.

It was far more pleasant this way. He flexed his hips against her and her breath caught.

"*Oh…*"

"Good *oh* or bad *oh?*"

"Definitely good. But Nico," she said, a note of worry creeping into her voice.

"Yes?"

"I'm not sure I can do this again tonight. It's, um, it's been a while."

He tried not to react, but he felt his body stiffen as he wondered exactly when the last time for her was. And who it was with. "I understand, *cara.*"

"Do you?" she said, her hand resting on his cheek. "Because that felt a lot like you didn't."

He turned into her palm, kissed it. "Has it been very long since the last time?"

She laughed. "Yeah, two years."

He stilled. Blinked. She could not be telling him what he thought she was telling him. "I don't think I heard you correctly."

She kissed his chin. "You did. You're the only man I've ever been with."

A fierce feeling of satisfaction permeated his entire being. She was his, had only ever been his. "How is this possible?" he asked. "*Sei bellisima,* Liliana. Any man would kill to have you."

"I never found another one I wanted," she said very softly.

"You do me much honor," he replied, uncertain what else he could say to express how grateful he was for the gift of her innocence and trust two years ago, and for her confession now. It was primitive of him, but he liked knowing she'd only been his.

She laughed. "Oh, Nico, you make it sound like we're living in the Middle Ages or something. For a man who knows how to do the things you do with your tongue, you sound awfully formal and prudish just now."

"Do I?" He grinned at her. "Perhaps I should remind you how wicked I can be, yes? I'm sure I can think of a few things that won't abuse your tenderness."

"I'm counting on it," she said breathlessly as he rolled her to her back and began another thorough exploration of her delightful body.

Lily had no idea what time she awoke, but when she did she found that Nico had made her breakfast again—only this time he served it in bed. When she finished eating, he ran her a bath in the gorgeous sunken tub, shedding his wet clothes to join her after she playfully splashed him.

She climbed on his lap, facing him, her legs wrapped around him and their bodies touching in that most intimate of places. He was engorged, ready for her, yet he made no move to enter her in spite of the way she rubbed against him.

Instead, he held her gently, grabbed a sponge and squeezed it over her breasts. Her nipples were tight little points that seemed to tighten even more when the air drifted over her wet body.

"*Dio santo,* you are beautiful," he said.

She wasn't, but she loved to hear him say it. Loved him, in fact. How had she committed such a colossal mistake? She had no idea, but she didn't care. She was in love with the man she was bound to for life. How bad could it be? He could learn to love her eventually, she was sure of it.

He was *not* like her father. Nico had honor and dignity. He loved their son, he cherished her body, and he felt deeply about many things. He was a man capable of love; he would not abandon her to raise their son alone, would not leave her for long stretches of time and then return and ask to be forgiven only to repeat the entire cycle in a few months or years.

Would he?

No, of course not.

"You're beautiful, too," she said, reaching beneath the water to wrap her hand around him.

His breath caught. "You are insatiable, *cara.* I quite like it," he finished, dropping the sponge and fusing his mouth to hers. While he kissed her, she managed to wriggle herself up high enough that the tip of him nudged her entrance. She caught his moan in her mouth, then gave it back to him when he thrust the rest of the way inside her.

"I am yours, Liliana," he said brokenly. "Do with me what you will."

Hers.

She'd never felt more powerful in her life as she began to move her hips. His head tilted back on the edge of the tub, his eyes drifted closed, and joy suffused her. She rode him slowly at first, drawing out the torment for them both. But then she needed more, so much more. Water sloshed over the rim of the tub to soak the tile, but he didn't seem to care.

And, oh God, neither did she.

"Nico," she gasped as her body began to shudder. *No, not yet.*

She changed the angle, slowed her thrusts. But he caught her hips tight, held her in such a way that she took him deeper with each thrust.

His eyes opened, burning into her. Burning *for* her.

"Take me, Lily. Take all of me," he growled.

This man, this gorgeous beautiful prince, was in ecstasy because of *her,* because of what she did to him. It amazed her, and humbled her. And sent her tumbling over the edge far too quickly when she wanted to drag it out forever.

"Nico," she cried as she shattered. "Nico, oh, I…" *I love you.*

Her heart was full with all she felt and could not say. It was too new, too raw, and she wasn't yet sure how to deal with it. He held her rigid when she would have folded against him and drove into her again and again, drawing out the pleasure for them both. When she came a second time, he was with her, his groan mingling with her sharp cry.

"I'm sorry, Lily. Don't cry," he said long moments later when her heart rate had almost returned to normal. He held her gently, fingers dancing up and down her spine. "It is my fault. I should not have made love to you again so soon. You make me lose control when I should know better."

She reached up to touch her cheeks, realized they were moist with tears. "Oh. No, I'm fine, really. It's just so... overwhelming."

"*Si,* it is that," he said, tucking a lock of her damp hair behind her ear. "There have been many changes for you."

That wasn't what she meant, but how could she tell him?

"And for you." She cupped his face in her hands. "I'm sorry, Nico. I should have contacted you when I found out I was pregnant. I made a mistake."

His gaze was troubled, but then it seemed to pass. "We will have to make another baby, yes? A little brother or sister for Daniele."

Lily's heart ached with love and a feeling of rightness. "He would like that. *I* would like that," she finished somewhat shyly considering what had just happened between them.

Nico's grin was genuine. "It is my solemn mission, *cara.* I shall rise to the occasion—just as soon as I recover from this one."

They returned to the city that afternoon, the journey seeming to weigh on Nico with every mile. The closer they got, the less he spoke, the less he smiled, the less he seemed the same man to her. Lily concentrated on the white buildings and red roofs in the distance, feeling as if Castello del Bianco were a tangible force drawing the life from her husband. And she didn't know how to fix it.

By the time they reached the Palazzo Cavelli, he'd returned to the coolly arrogant prince she'd thought was gone forever. It confused and irritated her. What had happened to the effortlessly sensual man she'd had a bath with this morning? The man who'd shared his body and his soul with her, cooked her breakfast and slept with a toddler on his chest?

This man, this prince, was not the sort of person who would do any of those things.

Had she judged him wrongly once more? Had she made him into what she wanted him to be when in fact he only did what was expedient to his wishes?

He didn't stick around for long once they were inside their apartment. He said he had to meet with the king, then left without so much as a smile or a kind word. Lily stared at the closed door for long minutes after he'd gone. Fear, anger and hurt mixed in her stomach, pounded through her with the refrain that she wasn't really a princess, that she'd given her heart to a man who didn't love her in return, and that she'd lost any chance she'd ever had at happiness when she'd married him. He'd taken her career, such as it was, her baby and her heart.

After Lily checked on Danny, she retreated to the room she now shared with Nico. The opulence of the palace no longer staggered her, but still her breath caught at the magnificent antique bed, the gilded walls and plush furniture, the marble and crystal and priceless paintings. It was like living in a museum. She, who'd only been to a single art museum in her life, now lived in the middle of one.

It only added to her Alice-in-Wonderland confusion.

A knock on the door sounded and she turned toward it, almost grateful for the interruption.

"Yes?" she said, and then wondered if there was something else she was supposed to say. What did princesses say? *You may enter?*

A young woman in the palace staff uniform entered, her eyes downcast. "*Scusi, Principessa.* For you," she finished, holding out a box.

"*Grazie,*" Lily replied. The girl shot her a wary smile, then backed out of the room and closed the door.

Lily went over to a table and pulled the lid off the box. She lifted out a stack of newspapers and magazines, confused as to why they'd been sent to her.

Until she realized that it was *her* picture in a grainy news photo. The paper was in Italian, so she shuffled through until she found something she understood:

Crown Prince Marries Daughter of Alcoholic Stripper, Endangers Relations with Neighbor

By the time Nico made it back to his quarters, he was mentally exhausted. He'd spent the last several hours wrangling with King Paolo and his father over the state of the treaty between their nations.

Paolo had at first demanded he divorce Lily, repudiate his son and marry Antonella. The man was insane and Nico didn't mind saying so. His father, however, urged a different course. Paolo was posturing for the best deal he could and using whatever ammunition he had in his arsenal to get it. The public humiliation of his daughter was fairly substantial in his mind, though it would never have escalated to this point had he not bandied it in the press. Nico felt sorry for Antonella, but only because her father was a self-important fool. She was a beautiful woman and would command many offers for her hand once her father let this go.

Now, Paolo wanted to hold further talks about the treaty in Monteverde. Nico didn't want to go, but his father urged him to do so. As Crown Prince, it was his duty. As architect of the current impasse, it was his responsibility. He could hardly refuse the invitation. To be seen in Monteverde, with his wife, would go a long way toward normalizing relations. It would show that Montebianco needed Monteverde's goodwill, and it would give Paolo a chance to appear both important and magnanimous.

The residence was quiet when he entered. He wasn't as late as he'd thought he might be, though perhaps Lily had gone to bed. Nico headed for the bedroom, anticipation pumping through his veins. Would his wife be naked in their bed, waiting for him? Would she be dressed in something slinky and enticing? Or would she be wearing that silly shirt with the cat on it?

It didn't matter which garment she wore—or didn't wear—because his reaction was the same with each image in his head. He wanted her, plain and simple.

But when he opened the door, the sight he found was not what he'd hoped for.

Papers littered the floor. Lily sat in the center of them, reading. She looked up at him, her eyes red. "Hullo, Nico. Have a good day at the office?"

He crossed over and snatched a paper off the floor. Fury settled into his bones like a permanent chill when he realized what these were. He would make whoever did this pay. An upended box lay under the table, and he knew that someone had saved everything until they'd returned.

Queen Tiziana, no doubt. It was just like her to be so heartless. The more innocent the victim, the crueler she could be. Her treatment of him had changed in proportion to his size and age, but when he'd first arrived, he'd been fresh meat. Just as Lily was. If the queen outlived his father, she would be lucky if Nico didn't banish her from the kingdom entirely.

He'd known there would be articles, but he'd avoided the papers during their honeymoon. He regretted it now. He was so accustomed to shrugging off what they said that he hadn't stopped to think he might need to prepare his wife better.

Obviously, he'd been wrong.

"They know *everything*," Lily said numbly. "My mother, my father—the town I grew up in, the fact our family took public assistance, that my mother once stripped for a living. They called me a gold digger, said I tricked you, that Danny isn't yours—"

"I know Danny is mine."

She waved the paper she was holding. "Yes, well maybe you'd like to tell them that? Issue a statement perhaps?"

"It does no good to answer these swine," he bit out.

She climbed to her feet, faced him squarely. Fury, he was surprised to see, was the dominant emotion. "I don't know how to do this, Nico. I'm not a princess. I'm not meant for this. I won't let them hurt Danny—"

"No one will hurt Danny," he vowed.

"Then you will make them retract these lies?"

"Montebianco is a free society, Lily. I can't make them do anything. Nor can I make the European gossip rags do what I wish, either. The best course is to ignore them."

She looked stunned. "Ignore them? You would ignore people calling your son a bastard and your wife a whore?"

Nico stiffened. "*I'm* a bastard, *cara*. And I assure you it makes no difference. The furor will die down soon enough. You are the Crown Princess now, you must learn to handle these things."

"I didn't realize that part of the *job* was learning to ignore lies and put up with insults."

"You worked for a newspaper," he said harshly. "How can this surprise you?"

"I worked with reporters who had integrity, Nico. No one would dare to print a lie that was easily disproved. It isn't professional."

Nico raked a hand through his hair. "Yes, well tabloids

don't have the same standards. They thrive on lies, the more outrageous the better."

She gaped at him. "How can you be so dismissive? It's embarrassing to me, but it makes *you* look incompetent."

"You are missing the point, Lily. It doesn't matter. It will go away tomorrow, or the next day. As soon as there's nothing left to feed on, they will move on to another target." He reached for her. "Come, let's go to bed and forget this. It will look better in the morning."

She jerked away. "I can't believe you would allow an insult to our son to go unchallenged. Of course I don't expect you to defend me, but—"

"There's nothing to defend," he roared. "*Cavolo,* I don't have time for this! We are flying to Monteverde tomorrow. I need you to be prepared."

She wrapped her arms around herself, looked away. Her chin quivered and guilt speared him. Perhaps he should be more patient, should help her through this with more compassion. He'd had a bad afternoon, but that was no excuse. "Lily—"

"Monteverde?" she cut in. "Isn't that where Princess Antonella lives?"

"*Si.*"

Her laugh was unexpected. "Fabulous, just fabulous. What if I refuse?"

Cold anger flooded him. "You cannot refuse. It's your duty."

"No, it's *your* duty."

Nico stiffened. "You are my wife, Liliana. We *will* be in Monteverde tomorrow night, and *you* will appear to be happy about it."

"Of course, Your Supreme Majesty," she bit out. "Is there anything else you wish to command, oh Lord of Everything?"

"Lily," he said, unable to keep the sudden weariness from his voice.

She sucked in a breath, her chin quivering faster now. He knew it wasn't from weakness, but from anger that she cried. "I didn't ask for *any* of this, Nico. I'm here because you forced me to be here. You've tried to turn me into something I'm not. If you don't like how I do the job of being your wife, then you have only yourself to blame for making a poor choice."

Nico gritted his teeth. "I did not force you to give me your virginity two years ago, nor did I rip the condom so you would get pregnant. It happened, Lily. Now we deal with it."

She made a sweeping motion with her hand. "So this is how we deal with it? Ignore the lies and hope they'll go away? Have you stopped to think what might happen when they actually manage to track my mother down in whatever third-rate honky-tonk dive she's holding up a bar stool in and ask her how it feels to have a daughter marry a prince?"

"They won't find her."

She went very still. "What do you mean they won't find her?"

"Because I found her first. She's in a treatment facility."

She looked as if he just said he'd sold her mother into slavery. But of course he'd had her family investigated. And what he'd learned about her mother necessitated action. The woman had been drunk in a Baton Rouge nightclub when his people found her. And, contrary to Lily's belief, she was most certainly still stripping for a living. Once she'd sobered, she couldn't even remember her grandson's name. Had, in fact, insisted she wasn't old enough to be a grandmother.

"You sent my mother to rehab? Without telling me?" He watched as a range of emotions crossed her face. Her voice sounded hollow when she spoke. "I haven't talked with her since shortly after Danny was born. How did you find her? Why?"

"I have many resources. And I had to do something for precisely the reason you've stated."

"I wanted to help her, but she never would listen and I

didn't have the money…." He had no idea what she might do next, but she suddenly gave up the fight and crumpled into a nearby chair. "You've thought of everything, haven't you? I should have known you would."

"I have no choice, Lily. I must do what's best for Montebianco at all times."

"Maybe you should have thought of that before you married me."

"There was no choice in that, either. I married you because we have a child together."

She laughed, but the sound was broken. Then she swiped her fingers beneath her eyes. "Not the best criteria, was it? But duty called, I suppose."

He resented the way she made it sound as if he'd committed a crime. He'd done what was right. And he'd done it at a personal cost that was still being tallied. "Yes."

"I wish you'd considered how it would affect me and Danny before you imposed your royal will."

His brows drew together. What could he have done differently? He'd given them wealth and privilege and a life far removed from what it would have been. "Your lives are immeasurably better now that we are married."

She speared him with a watery gaze. "Oh yes, very much so. I've never been happier."

In spite of her sarcasm, he wanted to go to her, wanted to sweep her up and take her to bed and make this whole thing go away. Because she had been happy just a few hours ago— he'd have staked everything he had on it.

But she wouldn't welcome him with open arms, not like this morning. It bothered him more than he cared to admit.

He went and picked up the phone, gave orders for someone to come clean up the mess.

"Go to bed, Lily," he said over his shoulder. "Tomorrow will be a long day."

She didn't answer for a long minute. When she did, her voice was so soft he had to strain to hear. But he didn't miss a word.

"I liked the man I knew in New Orleans, the one I spent the last few days with. Where is he? Because I don't like the Crown Prince very much at all."

Nico swallowed a hard knot in his throat. Was he so different when he was here in the palace? He knew he felt more constrained, but he'd not thought he completely submerged his personality beneath the pomp and circumstance of his duty. Perhaps he did. Perhaps she was far more perceptive than he.

"I am the same man," he said without turning around.

"I wish that were true. But I don't believe it is."

A few moments later, he heard papers shifting and crinkling as she stood and walked across the floor. A door closed. For the longest time, he heard nothing else. And then the snick of the lock fell into place.

The next day was a whirlwind of activity. Lily welcomed the distraction. She was caught in a flurry of fittings and beauty appointments to prepare for the gathering at the Romanellis' residence in Monteverde later that night. Unlike the trip to Paris, these women came to the palace to attend her. Gisela brought Danny in from time to time, and he amused the ladies to no end with his baby chatter and adorable antics. Lily was gratified by the comments that he looked exactly like his father.

Of course he did. Anyone with eyes could see he was his father's child, and yet she was still angry with Nico for refusing to correct the tabloids. When she'd worked at the *Register,* people sent in corrections to stories all the time. And the paper printed them.

She'd thought she wanted to be a journalist someday, but now she knew that was impossible. And she'd realized, after last night, that she really didn't have the necessary bulldog attitude it required. Some of what the papers said was true—her mother's alcohol addiction, the fact she'd once been a stripper—but Lily would never be able to write something so cruel and see it published if it meant someone would be hurt by it.

She'd been lulled by her short time at the *Register* into thinking that all papers and all stories were like the ones in her hometown. Naive of her, she knew. Especially now. She was news, and whatever a reporter could dig up about her was fair game. No wonder Nico was so jaded about fighting back.

But when he had right on his side, she refused to understand how he couldn't fight the battles that mattered. She didn't so much care about herself, though it hurt that Nico wouldn't defend her, but Danny, her sweet baby—he did not deserve the aspersions on his parenthood.

It had infuriated her to read them. This morning, she'd asked for the papers to be delivered to her. She'd thought Nico might have issued orders to the contrary, but within moments a maid brought all the English language papers she could find. The articles had thinned somewhat, though there was a picture of her and Nico on the motorcycle. And a grainier one of them and Danny on the beach.

She scanned the articles, then bunched the papers up and stuffed them in the trash. Privacy was no longer a guarantee. It would take getting used to, but she would survive it, same as she'd survived everything else in her life. It would take more than a few negative stories to defeat her.

By the time evening fell, Lily hadn't seen Nico all day. When she'd gone to bed last night, she'd locked the door. She'd been angry, and maybe she'd behaved childishly, but she hadn't expected him to avoid her completely. She'd spent a very lonely night awake on cool sheets, aching for the man she loved and dying inside because he wasn't the person she'd begun to think he was.

He'd married her for Danny. She wasn't stupid; she'd known it was the truth. And yet, to hear him say it so baldly, so blandly—it squeezed her heart into a tiny ball. She'd done everything wrong. She'd meant to insulate her heart from him, meant to learn how to live with him without falling for him—but she'd failed.

And now she was paying for it. Was this what her mother had felt all those years? This aching emptiness that could only be filled by one man? Maybe so, but she would not be the woman her mother had been. Danny was her priority. Nico did not care about her, so she would not expend her energy agonizing over him.

She would do her *duty*, but that was all. She would go to Monteverde and smile as though she was the happiest princess in the world.

After she was dressed, she awaited Nico in the living area. She'd been gowned in the most exquisite silver dress that hugged her curves from breast to ankle. The dress had a small train, and she'd been fitted with a sash like the one he'd worn the first night she came to the palace. Long white gloves went up to her elbows, and a diamond tiara perched on her head. She'd stared at herself in the mirror for long minutes, unable to believe the sight of all those diamonds winking like a neon sign.

When she was eight, she'd had a cheap plastic tiara with paste jewels that her mother had gotten from a thrift store. She'd shut the door to her room and pretend to be a princess, waltzing with her prince at a grand ball. Every night, until the tiara disappeared in one of their moves. She'd cried for a week. That her life should now imitate her childhood dreams was too surreal.

But in her dreams, the prince loved her. Too bad reality was so different.

When Nico entered the room, her heart leaped at the sight of him. He was resplendent in the ceremonial uniform of the Montebiancan navy. Though he had the sash and medals, this time the sword was missing. He drew up short when he saw her.

"Sei belissima, Principessa," he said.

Lily clasped her trembling hands together. She'd had protocol lessons today, but she had to admit she was nervous about this evening. "Thank you. I think."

He smiled as if nothing bad had happened between them. "It means you are beautiful."

She dropped her gaze to the floor, swallowed. She couldn't look at him and pretend nothing was wrong.

"You are prepared for this?" he asked.

Lily lifted her head. "Yes. I will do my duty, Nico."

She didn't have to wonder if he heard the bitter twist she put on the word. Something sparked in his eyes—but was it guilt or resentment?

Or neither?

He held out his arm for her in silence. She took it and they headed for their waiting helicopter. She was beginning to understand that she really didn't know him at all, no matter what they might have shared.

He'd married her for Danny's sake. But if duty demanded it, would he divorce her just as quickly?

CHAPTER TEN

THERE WERE THREE KINGDOMS, Lily learned on the flight to Monteverde's capital, that had once been a single country. But more than a thousand years ago, three feuding brothers divided the country between them when their father died. Montebianco, Monteverde and Monterosso were now ruled by the descendents of those brothers—though the connection was so far in the past they were no longer related except in the most distant way.

Montebianco and Monterosso had good diplomatic ties, and had done for over one hundred years now. But Monteverde was the odd kingdom out, the one ruled by a tyrant who controlled his people's access to news, the Internet and travel. They were an insular people, but they had many things to offer if free trade could be established. The Monterossan king refused to negotiate with King Paolo, but Montebianco was the peacemaker of the three. Good relations, Nico explained, would benefit everyone.

Lily had never ridden in a helicopter, but she had a feeling this one did not quite count. The interior was plush, like Nico's jet, lined with cushioned seats and polished wood. "Marrying me ruined everything, didn't it?" she asked when he'd finished his discourse on regional politics.

His expression didn't change. "It did not please Paolo, no."

She wondered if he regretted his hasty decision to marry her, but she could not bring herself to ask it right now. She'd been angry last night, and she'd as good as said that her life would have been better if he hadn't forced her into marriage.

And yet she wasn't certain it was the truth. Yes, she'd have her independence—but she wouldn't have the freedom to be the kind of mother she'd been lately, the sort of mother who had the luxury to spend as much time with her baby as she wanted. She'd still be working long hours to provide a good home for them both and wondering when life would ever get easier. Her baby would be spending most of his time in day care instead of with her. Though Nico had taken much from her, he'd also given her a precious gift. If he said that he regretted it, she wasn't sure how she would handle it.

Instead, she turned to the window and watched the darkness slide by until the lights of a city appeared on the horizon. Once they arrived at the seaside fortress belonging to Monteverde's king, their six-man security team, clad in black suits and probably packing enough artillery to take over a small country, preceded Nico and Lily out of the helicopter and took up stations to await their descent. Nico went first, then held out his hand and helped Lily to the landing pad.

A man in a white dinner jacket and bow tie came forward and bowed deeply. "Serene Highnesses, welcome."

Lily bit the inside of her lip and followed Nico's lead. She had to relax, had to get through this night and the inevitable meeting with Princess Antonella so that she could return to the palace and hug her baby close again.

Would she lock the bedroom door tonight? Or should she encourage Nico to join her? She was still angry with him, but perhaps they could move forward if they reconnected on the intimate level they'd shared at his house on the beach.

"Relax, Lily," Nico said quietly, looping her arm inside his and placing his hand over hers. "You are the Crown Princess of Montebianco. You outrank everyone here with the exception of the king. Remember this when you feel overwhelmed."

"I just want it over with," she said through the smile she'd pasted on her face as they passed between two rows of onlookers on the portico.

"It will be so soon enough," he said as they entered the interior.

Not soon enough for her liking.

They stopped in front of a large set of double doors, and the man who'd escorted them spoke to Nico in Italian. When he was finished, Nico bent to whisper in her ear.

"They will announce us, and we will enter onto the ceremonial staircase. We stand while the photographers take our picture, and then we descend. The king is not yet in attendance, but will appear after we've arrived."

"So we don't upstage him?"

"Precisely, *cara*."

Somehow, she got through the grand entrance, the photos, and then down the stairs—without stumbling on her high heels—to a large ballroom that had fewer people than she'd expected. It wasn't empty, but it wasn't packed, either.

Nico handed her a champagne flute. She took it, but did not drink. If anything, she needed a clear head tonight. They did not have long to wait before King Paolo arrived. He was a large, florid man, dressed in a uniform that was dripping with jewels and medals. At his side was a woman who made Lily's heart stutter in her chest.

Princess Antonella was the most graceful, elegant creature she'd ever seen. Her long, thick hair was swept into a pile on her head; her tiara made Lily's look puny, and she wore a deep ruby gown that set off her hair and skin to perfection. She walked with a lush, sensual roll of her hips that was most surely designed to rivet the attention of any male within sight. Lily wanted desperately to look at Nico, to see if there was regret or lust on his face, but to turn away would be an insult to the king.

And perhaps it was a blessing she couldn't look at Nico. Was she truly prepared to handle what she saw there?

Instead, she focused on the couple coming down the stairs. Antonella's beautiful face was set in a cool, detached mask while the king looked gruff and arrogant. From the corner of her eye, Lily saw Nico bend at the waist. At the last second, she remembered to drop into a curtsy.

"Welcome to Monteverde, Your Highness," King Paolo said to Nico, ignoring her altogether.

"We are delighted to be here, Your Majesty," Nico replied smoothly, though she knew it was anything but the truth. "My wife and I thank you for your hospitality."

"Come then, let me introduce you to some of my government ministers," the king said to Nico. "Antonella, entertain the prince's companion."

Lily watched them go, her heart pounding so hard she thought everyone could surely see it, and then turned to the woman who would have been Nico's wife had it not been for her. She expected to see hatred, but Antonella's expression remained cool and controlled. "*Principessa,* do join me."

She led the way to a small sitting area off one end of the ballroom. A few other women occupied the space, but found a reason to leap up and fade into the background as soon as Lily and Antonella appeared.

Lily sank onto a chair facing her beautiful rival. "I'm sorry you have to do this."

How hard it must be for Antonella to have to entertain her in public, knowing everyone was watching her be nice to the woman who'd ruined her happiness.

Antonella raised her champagne glass. "It is my duty," she replied before taking a delicate sip.

That word again. Lily was beginning to hate the sound of

it. She turned her head sideways, studying the other woman. Something about her makeup…

"Are you okay?"

Antonella shifted in her seat, rotating the right side of her face away from scrutiny. "Yes. It is nothing," she said, her fingers straying up to her cheek. "I was clumsy and ran into a door."

It was possible, Lily supposed, but she didn't quite buy it. Still, the bruise under Antonella's eye was none of Lily's business. It was well hidden under her makeup, though upon closer inspection the purpling skin was obvious when compared with the left side of her face.

Who would hit her? Her father? The idea horrified Lily, but then she'd disliked the man on sight—and Nico's description of him hadn't exactly been warm.

But Antonella seemed uncomfortable, so Lily didn't mention it again. The minutes ticked by as Antonella made small talk, and Lily soon relaxed. She found she couldn't help but like the princess even if the other woman was so well schooled in proper behavior that her questions were merely polite and not truly because she was interested.

"Your son, he is talking now?"

Lily laughed. "He talks quite a lot, yes."

"I think I would like a baby someday," she said almost wistfully.

Lily bit her lip and leaned forward. She hesitated to speak, but decided she had to do it. For her own peace of mind, if nothing else. "I'm sorry if I've caused you pain. But I'm not sorry Nico chose to be a father to his son."

Antonella's exotic eyes widened. "You love him?"

She'd gone this far; there was nothing for it except to be honest. The feeling was still so raw and new, but she wanted to share it with someone. Was it wrong to do so with this woman who had loved him, too? Or was it right to let Antonella know where she stood? "Yes, I do."

"Then I am very glad for you. To be in love, it is extraordinary. I wish to feel this for a man someday." Antonella's smile was startling—and genuine.

Lily blinked. "You aren't in love with Nico?"

"Oh good heavens, no," she laughed.

Lily felt as if a weight had been lifted from her soul. Antonella did not love Nico!

"You seem quite pleased," the princess said, smiling once more.

"I have to admit I am. I was afraid I'd ruined all your dreams." But what about Nico? Had he been in love with Antonella? She didn't think so—but she wasn't certain. It seemed unlikely. Or did it?

Antonella shook her head. "I was engaged to Gaetano first. Poor man. He chose his path, and that is all any of us can hope to do—though not so tragically, one would hope. When Gaetano died, my father negotiated to wed me to Nico instead."

Lily remembered her conversation with Antonella in Paris. She'd said she had a habit of chasing away grooms. Now it made sense.

"You *will* find someone," Lily said. "It'll happen when you least expect it, I imagine."

Antonella frowned. "I am not so sure. Love is perhaps not for me." Her gray eyes were piercing suddenly. "Be careful, Lily. Prince Nico, he is handsome and pleasing, but he knows these things about himself. He knows how to make women love him. He also knows how to break hearts."

Lily realized she was clutching her hands in her lap. "I—yes, I know."

Antonella reached across and squeezed her hand. "I do not wish to upset you. You are a nice girl, but Nico is a jaded man. I would not say this if I didn't know the truth. He had an affair with one of my school friends a few years ago. She'd been expecting marriage, I think. But Nico found a new woman to amuse himself with and moved on. This is often the way with such men."

"Such men?" Lily repeated, feeling the twist of the vise around her heart with every word.

"He is a prince, gifted with a handsome face and raised on entitlement. Trust me, I have a brother. I understand this quite well. But do not fret yourself, Lily! Nico may very well be tamed by marriage, and I will have upset you for nothing."

"No, you're right. I'd be naive to think otherwise." Lily sipped her champagne because she needed something to do. The liquid was no longer cold, and the bubbles nearly made her sneeze.

Perhaps she'd need to take champagne-drinking lessons before the next official soiree, she thought sourly. The idea would have made her laugh had her conversation with Antonella not tweaked that insecure part of her that was simply waiting for Nico to live up to his playboy reputation.

And what did she expect anyway? It'd been a little under two weeks since he'd married her, only a couple of days since they'd started having sex. Did she really think he could feel the same for her as she did for him? That his fascination with her body was anything more than the excitement of being with a new lover?

Until last night, he'd said all the right things, complimented her and seemed to enjoy their lovemaking. But was that enough to build a real relationship on? Without Danny, the entire scenario would be moot. He would not have lifted a single custom-shod foot to tromp down to her cell in the police station if she hadn't been carrying a picture of her baby. It was enough to make her breath catch painfully.

Antonella's gaze went beyond Lily's shoulder, her expression morphing from confusion to horror. Lily pivoted in her chair to see what was going on. A group of men in uniform, carrying automatic rifles, stomped toward them. Antonella bolted to her feet. Lily joined her more out of instinct than anything, surprised when the other woman gripped her hand and moved her body in front of Lily as if to shield her.

"What do you want?" Antonella demanded when the men fanned out, taking up position around them.

"Scusi, Principessa Antonella," a tall, lean man who seemed to be the group leader said. "But we are under orders to take this woman into custody."

"This *woman*," Antonella pronounced, "is the Crown Princess of Montebianco. Surely you are mistaken."

"No, *Mi Principessa,* I am not."

Nico sat in the king's private study, listening to the man expound on his theory of a united Monteverde and Montebianco forcing Monterosso to bow to their collective wills. It was entertaining, if pointless. The man had despotic tendencies and ambitions that were no good for his country, especially if he truly attempted to put any of his plans into action.

Nico had been introduced to several government ministers, who were only yes-men to Paolo, and then shown to the king's study where Paolo insisted he share a vintage bottle of Montebiancan brandy and talk.

Or, as it turned out, listen.

Nico was more than ready to leave. He glanced at his watch. Another minute, and he was making his excuses, retrieving his wife and flying home. He'd already been here two hours and Paolo had yet to commit to any of his proposals for getting the treaty back on track.

Maybe Nico's heart wasn't in it. He'd been out of sorts since his argument with Lily last night. He'd wanted to go to her, wanted to bust down the door and make love to her until she screamed his name, but he hadn't been able to make himself act. She'd said he'd made her life worse by forcing her into marriage. And he'd wanted to rail at her that in contrast he'd made *his* life worse. He was the one justifying his actions to his father, to this irritating man pontificating about alliances and the future, and to himself as he began to wonder whether he'd done the right thing or not.

He'd never wanted a child of his to endure a life like the one he'd had, but had marriage been the necessary vehicle to take care of Danny? Could he not have found another way to provide for them?

Basta, no. He'd done the right thing, the *only* thing he could do. Lily would learn how to be a princess, and Danny would grow up as a prince and the heir to the throne. What was done was done.

A man came in to hand Paolo a paper, leaning over to whisper something in his ear as he did so. Paolo's face split into a grin.

"Prince Nico," Paolo said when the man had gone again. "It seems as if we have caught a thief."

"A thief? How extraordinary."

Paolo's mouth twitched. "Indeed, she is quite extraordinary."

Nico's skin prickled in warning.

"I am so sorry to inform you, Your Highness, but it seems as if the woman who accompanied you tonight is part of an international gang of antiquities thieves."

Nico shot out of the chair just as the door burst open to admit several armed men. He stood there in impotent rage, fists clenched at his side, heart racing, and glared at the man who watched him with an amused look on his face.

"If you've hurt her—"

How could he have brought her here tonight? How could he have put her in danger? He should have refused, no matter what his father or Paolo demanded. Ice dripped into his veins. He needed to deal with this man coldly, on his level. He could not afford the distraction of *any* emotion right now.

"This is what you will do," Paolo said coolly, all pretence

gone. "You will divorce this woman and marry my daughter, as you should have done in the first place."

"You dare to imprison my wife? To threaten me? You're risking war, Paolo."

"You would take your country to war over a woman? Like Menelaus, yes? You know what happened to Menelaus—the beautiful Helen ran off with Paris willingly, and the Greeks spent ten years trying to get her back. Was it worth it?"

"It's not about the woman," he bit out. "It's about sovereignty. You insult my nation with this act of aggression against her Crown Prince."

Paolo's face turned an alarming shade of purple as he banged a fist on his desk. His crystal tumbler rattled violently, brandy sloshing over the side to splash the wood.

"You *will* marry my daughter. I insist on it. I have worked too hard to be thwarted by one such as you." Spittle formed at the corners of his mouth. "If you don't do as I say, I will have you both killed."

Nico was tempted to laugh—until he realized Paolo meant the threat. The man's eyes gleamed with barely contained madness. He'd thought Paolo was simply stubborn before, but it was much more than that. The King of Monteverde was unbalanced. There'd been rumors to that effect for a few years now, but there were always rumors coming out of royal palaces. He knew that firsthand, which was why he'd given them little credence.

Nico sized up the man before him. He could resist, but what was the point? If he agreed to do what Paolo wanted, then he had a chance to save Lily. Because he would not allow her to remain here as Paolo's prisoner—even if he had to die to free her. He'd put her in danger, he would get her out again.

"Very well, Your Majesty. But I want to see Lily first. And I want your assurance she will be well treated."

* * *

That this cell was far more luxurious than the one in which she'd been imprisoned in Montebianco was not a comfort. Bars were bars, and guards were guards.

Lily wrapped her arms around herself and stood in the middle of the sumptuously appointed room, an actual palace room with a cell door welded to the frame. Very odd, but then she'd learned that nothing was as she expected it to be since she'd left Port Pierre. Part of her could hardly believe she was here. Another part wanted to howl.

The lean man with the blade-thin nose had told her she was under arrest for her ties to an international ring of thieves who dealt in artifacts. The idea was preposterous, and yet here she was.

She rubbed her gloved hands over her bare shoulders. The chill ricocheting over her skin was the result of bone-deep fear, not from a lack of warmth in her prison. No, the room was everything a guest could want—were she a guest.

Lily sniffed back angry tears. This was all a mistake. She had faith that Nico would fix it. He would not allow his wife to be imprisoned by a neighboring monarch.

Antonella, bless her, had resisted mightily—but orders were orders and the guards were determined to carry them out. Lily finally agreed to go, certain it was a mistake and that it would all be sorted out.

When Nico finally appeared, relief threatened to buckle her knees. Lily flung herself at the bars, reaching for him. "Nico, what's going on? Get me out of here!"

She had only a glimpse of the fury on his face before he turned away from her as King Paolo came into view. Nico was coldly, brutally angry. If she were Paolo, she'd shrink in terror.

Yet the king merely looked smug. "You have seen her," he said in English, no doubt for her benefit. "Now you will return home and divorce her."

"Your word she will not be harmed, Paolo, or the deal is off."

The deal? "Nico? What's going on?"

He ignored her. A chill snaked down her spine, even colder than the chill she'd felt when she'd been brought to this room. Why was he so calm, so dispassionate? Didn't he care that she was in a cell? Or was he truly making deals with this awful man?

The possibility of it staggered her. And the truth. Montebianco came first. He'd told her that more than once. If he had to sacrifice her for his country, he would do so.

Oh God—

"She will not be harmed," Paolo said. Then he chortled gleefully. "Oh this is fun! I may have forgotten to mention, by the way, that I will soon have your son in my custody. Just in case you have any ideas of reneging on our agreement."

Lily's heart stopped. It. Just. Stopped.

How could she worry about herself when her baby was in danger? She wanted to choke the life from this man. From *both* of them. Fury, dark and cold, ate her from the inside out.

"If you hurt my child," she swore savagely, "I'll kill you myself."

Paolo spun toward her, laughing. "Oh ho, a threat to the monarch's life. This as well as her involvement with that despicable gang of thieves."

"You lying bastard," Lily hissed.

"Lily," Nico said sharply. "Enough."

"No," she shouted, gripping the bars in her fists. "How dare you stand there so passively when this—this *man* threatens our baby?" Her gaze swung to Paolo. "Tell me *right now* what you've done with my child!"

Paolo's glee was unholy. "Your nanny is a sweet creature, is she not? And yet she has a price. Everyone does—is that not right, Your Highness?" he asked Nico.

A muscle in Nico's jaw ticked, but he didn't reply. How could he stand there so mutely? She wanted to shake him, scream at him, *make* him act! He wouldn't correct the media, and now he wouldn't stop this evil king? What kind of man was he?

"Yes," Paolo said again, "everyone has a price. Mine is that you marry my daughter and make her your queen."

Lily felt as if someone had yanked the floor out from under her. She gripped the bars in an effort to hold herself up. Nico would not agree to this. *He would not, would not—*

"I have said I will do so," Nico replied. "But I want my son back immediately. Without him, there is no deal."

CHAPTER ELEVEN

SOMETIME DURING THE NIGHT, a team of black-clad men with face masks, night-vision goggles, headphones, and weapons burst through the outer doors to her prison and incapacitated the two guards. A voice ordered her to stand back, and then a flash of light split the gloom. Before she could process the popping sound, her cell door swung open and one of the men swept her into his arms.

Lily had no idea who they were or where they were taking her, but she prayed to God it was somewhere safe and that she would be reunited with her baby. She clung to her rescuer's neck, tired and aching and so, so ready for this nightmare to be over.

The men rushed up to the landing pad where a black helicopter descended onto the tarmac, blades whopping and doors wide-open. They piled in as shouts went up from below. Moments later, the craft levitated to the metallic burst of gunfire.

This helicopter was much louder than the executive version she'd flown in earlier, a stripped-down military monster that made conversation impossible. Lily tried to get away from the man still holding her, but his grip didn't loosen. As her struggle intensified, he reached up with one hand, stripped off the mask and headset and let them fall.

Lily's shock lasted only a second. Then she slapped him.

* * *

The city looked the same as it had yesterday, and yet nothing was the same. Lily refused to speak to him. Not that Nico blamed her. He sat at his desk staring into nothingness. He couldn't concentrate on the papers his assistant had given him earlier. The events of the night before had been outrageous, brutal and shocking. He'd wanted to strangle Paolo with his bare hands, yet to do so would have been a death sentence for them both.

Instead, he'd wasted no time once he'd left Monteverde in ordering Lily's rescue.

He shoved away from the desk and made his way to the nursery. He knew she would be there. She hadn't left their son's side since he'd brought her home. He hadn't wanted to leave, either, but his presence seemed to upset her. For the time being, he'd respected that. But no more.

Sunlight speared into the nursery. Danny was in his crib, napping. The sight of his son curled up with the blue dinosaur sent a wave of emotion through him. If not for the nanny's decision to do the right thing, he might have lost his wife and child both. A wave of despair tumbled through him at the thought.

A movement caught his eye and he turned his attention to the window. Lily lay on the window seat, head turned to look outside, a book dangling from one hand.

"Liliana," he said, surprised at how rough his voice sounded. At the mix of feelings tumbling through him. He shut them down without mercy, as he'd learned to do long ago. He already felt so out of sorts that he couldn't process them right now.

She turned bloodshot eyes on him. "Go away."

"No."

She didn't respond, simply stared out the window. He went to her side, took the book away and sat facing her, trapping her between him and the casing.

"Please don't touch me," she said, her voice cracking with the effort to control it.

"I apologize for what happened. I should have refused to take you to Monteverde. I did not trust Paolo, but I didn't know he was crazy enough to carry out such a scheme. He did not harm you, did he?"

She shook her head.

"Lily—*Dio*, I'm sorry you had to think I would go along with his plan, but it was the only way—"

"How did he get to Gisela?"

Nico shoved his fingers through his hair. "She has a brother, *tesoro mio*. He has been in much trouble in the past, and he'd once more fallen in with a gang. He disappeared a few days ago, no doubt on Paolo's orders. Gisela was offered money and the return of her brother should she hand Danny over when ordered. Instead, she chose to go to the authorities when the command came."

Wisely, since Paolo would have killed them both once he had Danny. Fortunately, Nico's men had located her brother; he was now free and would receive the rehabilitation he needed.

Her lip quivered. "I *am* grateful for that, but—oh God— he's just a baby. I wanted him to have a normal life, and now this. Will he always be at such risk?" Her head dropped to her knees as she brought them up in front of her, shielding her face from his view. "Of course he will, and it terrifies me. How do you live like this? Wait, don't tell me—*duty*."

"Nothing like this has ever happened before—"

She speared him with a glare. "But that doesn't mean it won't again! I thought the media was bad, but what if something happened to one of us? Or both of us? What would Danny do then? And if you tell me the king and queen would take care of him, I'll scream. Those two shouldn't be allowed to take care of a goldfish, much less a child—"

"Nothing will happen, Lily," he said firmly, though he

couldn't disagree with her assessment of the royal couple's child-rearing skills. "We have taken the men who were behind the thefts into custody, and many of the artifacts have been recovered. It was a Monteverdian gang that Paolo sanctioned in order to finance his greed. Some of the art had been lost along the way, which is how those statues ended up amongst the ones the vendor had. It's over now."

"Maybe this time—but what about the next?"

"There will be no next. Paolo was a desperate man, *cara.* He steered Monteverde into bankruptcy over the years of his rule. The union with Montebianco was necessary for him to infuse his failing government with cash, but it was his last resort. His son has challenged his rule and it looks like he will be removed from power. Then the healing will begin."

"Things like this don't happen where I come from. Life is *normal.*" She gave a half-hysterical laugh, sucked it in sharply. "My God, until last night, I had no idea you were actually in the military, that you would risk yourself in a rescue operation—"

"Did you think the uniform was simply for show?" he said gently. He wasn't an active member of the Montebiancan navy any longer, but he'd been trained extensively during his time in the service. He'd been advised against the mission because he was the Crown Prince, not because he wasn't prepared. Nothing, however, could have kept him from going.

"I don't know what I thought. But I do know I hate it here," she said softly, her eyes filling with tears again. "I've been nothing but miserable since the moment I set foot in this country—no, since the moment I met you two years ago." She pressed the heels of her hands to her eyes. "God, what an idiot I was to get involved with you."

"Then why did you do so? You should have given yourself to someone more worthy, then married him and bought your house and picket fence, as you Americans say."

Her comment stung, though he knew she wasn't wrong. Far better for her if he'd simply prevented the pickpocket from taking her purse and said goodbye. Instead, he'd been intrigued by her sweet innocence.

She shook her head. "I wish I had. I wish Danny was someone else's child."

If she'd pierced his heart with a hot knife, she couldn't have caused him more pain. But he knew something else now, something he should have recognized long ago.

"Lily, look at me. Please." He waited until she did so. The move was reluctant, but it was enough. "I should have told you who I was that night. I would say that I shouldn't have made love to you, but the truth is I don't regret that. If I'd realized in time, then yes, I should have stopped. But when I knew you were innocent, that I was your first, I should have been truthful with you."

He lifted his hand to touch her, thought better of it. "The first time is special, for a woman most of all I think. It is your right to know who you give yourself to."

Her shoulders slumped. "So many *shoulds,* Nico. Will we ever get it right?"

"Does anyone?"

"When there's love, then yes, I think so. But you don't love me. And I don't love you." She wouldn't look at him when she said it. Her words hurt him more than he'd have thought possible. She didn't love him. What did he feel?

His life was happier with her in it. But was that love? He didn't know, and couldn't focus on figuring it out when he was still smarting from the knowledge she didn't love him.

"I am fond of you, Lily. You have courage and integrity. You are the mother of my son, the mother of my future sons. We will have a good life together."

"But you *will* tire of me eventually. And then you'll go back to your mistresses and party-boy ways."

"I want no one but you," he protested, stung.

"Now. It will change, Nico. You're that kind of man."

He didn't know what to say, how to reach her. He just wanted to hold her, but he knew she would not let him right now. "Let us not talk about this yet. When the time comes, we will discuss—"

"When the time comes?" she hissed. She shoved herself up. The book fell to the floor with her sudden movement, but she ignored it. She popped her fists onto her hips and glared at him. "I thought you were out of your mind last night when you came bursting in with a group of commandos, but this absolutely takes the cake—"

Danny's cry interrupted her speech. She hurried to the crib, swung Danny into her arms and turned back to fix him with a hard look. "Go away, Nico. I don't want to talk to you right now."

Danny began to wail as she rocked him too hard. He saw the worry and self-loathing on her face, but then she seemed to take a deep breath—and calm washed over her. Danny's wailing turned softer as she crooned rhythmically.

Nico watched her soothe their son, something in him growing tight and heavy. She shot him another glare, then turned her back on him, shutting him out. Danny looked over her shoulder, but even he turned away without acknowledging his father.

Long after Nico was gone, Lily still wanted to walk out onto the terrace and scream at the top of her lungs. Maybe she would feel better. Most likely, however, she would make her throat hurt even worse than it already did. She'd yelled herself hoarse when Nico left her in the prison cell last night, then she'd cried when she thought she was doomed to stay there. She'd truly believed Nico had sacrificed her for his country's sake.

But, damn it, she was finished with crying. She had no one but herself to blame for the way she felt about him. She'd known what he was before she'd fallen in love with him. Why he'd risked himself in the rescue operation was beyond her. She did not fool herself he did it because of her.

She watched Danny play with a red fire truck and felt an urge to pick him up and hold him tight. She'd already done that so many times today that he was getting quite fussy whenever she gave in to the urge.

But she'd almost lost him, and it made her feel panicky and on edge. Still, she sat on her hands and watched him play, unable to leave him for more than a few moments at a time. Nico had already sent a new nanny—an older woman with a kindly smile—but Lily was reluctant to retreat for some much-needed rest.

Nothing about her life had been even remotely normal since the moment she'd arrived. She wasn't kidding Nico about that, though she'd perhaps been a bit harsh when she said that she wished Danny were someone else's child. She'd been upset, confused. She just wanted a normal life for her and her child. Why was that so much to ask?

"Oh God," she said, pressing her hands to her eyes again. She had to stop this weepiness. It was ridiculous.

He wasn't a bad man; he was a good man, a man with a strong belief in doing what was right. He'd married her so Danny would have a father, no other reason, and she had to admit it was noble—even if she didn't agree with his method or the fact she'd had no say in it once he decided. After his own childhood as the unwanted son under Queen Tiziana's thumb, she could understand why he did not scatter illegitimate children in the wake of his liaisons.

When he'd learned of Danny, he'd been truly shocked. Since then, he'd done the best he knew how to take care of them both. He was not at all the irresponsible womanizer he'd been made out to be in the media.

She was angry with him, angry with herself, but she'd been wrong to lash out at him the way she had.

And yet, in spite of the way she felt about him, she knew for an absolute fact that she could not live the kind of uncertain life he wanted to restrict her to. She couldn't share his bed, couldn't love him and bear his children, all the while knowing he didn't feel the same. That's why she'd lied and said she didn't love him. How could she give him that kind of power over her?

And how, if she did, would she be any different than her mother had been? She'd grown up watching her mother reorder her life—*ruin* her life—simply to accommodate a man she couldn't seem to stop loving no matter how he treated her.

Lily would not compromise herself that way. Not ever. And she intended to tell Nico that just as soon as she apologized for saying she'd been miserable since she'd met him.

"Signora Cosimo, can you watch Danny?" she said as she went into the adjoining room.

"*Si, Mi Principessa,*" the woman replied, curtsying deeply.

He'd made a mess of everything.

Basta! Nico threw down his pen and put his head in his hands. Why, in trying to do what was right, did he keep getting everything wrong?

He'd made a mistake in bringing Lily here. She was beautiful and vibrant, and she loved their son to distraction. And he'd nearly lost them both because *he* had put them in danger. By forcing her to be his wife, by claiming his son, he'd put their lives on the line. They weren't accustomed to this life. Danny was young and would learn, but was it fair to force Lily to be something she did not want to be?

He loved his child. And, though his feelings were in a

tangle he was having trouble sorting out accurately, he knew he felt something for Lily. It wasn't the same as what he felt for Danny, which was why he couldn't quite figure it out. But he cared for her, cared what happened to her—cared very much about her happiness.

She didn't love him. She'd told him so only hours ago. It still hurt.

What kind of a selfish bastard was he to ask her to give up her life for him? Weren't there other solutions? He had money, power and the ability to travel when and where he liked. If he let her go, could they work it out somehow?

He didn't want to let her go. An ugly, selfish part of him raged at the thought of not having her in his life. At the thought of some other man making her his wife. But after everything that had happened, he owed it to her to give *her* the choice. She deserved far better than he'd done by her thus far. She deserved happiness.

If it was the last thing he did, he would give it to her. No matter how much it hurt.

Reluctantly, and with a sharp pain piercing his chest, Nico picked up the phone.

"Liliana."

Lily turned her head, stomping down on the current of pain and joy she felt each time he entered the room.

She'd looked for him everywhere earlier, but his assistant informed her he'd gone out. Exhausted, she'd finally given in to the urge to nap. Once she awoke, she'd showered and changed, then she sat on the terrace and watched the white lights of a cruise ship in the distance. It wasn't dark yet, but the sun had set and ribbons of crimson and purple still stretched across the horizon.

"I've been waiting for you," she said. "Anselmo said you were gone on business earlier."

"*Si*, there has been much to attend to." He moved with the shuffling gait of someone who was physically exhausted. He dropped a folder on the table before falling into a chair across from her. Before she could say anything, he pushed the folder toward her.

Her mouth felt suddenly dry. "What's that?"

"The answer, I hope."

"Answer to what?"

He rubbed his forehead absently, fixed her with a look. "Sign those papers, *cara,* and our marriage is no more. I am setting you free."

Lily had to work very hard to sound normal. "Is this a joke?"

"Not at all." He flipped the folder open, took a pen from inside and clicked it. Laid it with the top facing her. "Sign, Lily, and you may go."

Anger, fear, despair—she felt them all. "You aren't taking my son away from me. I told you before that I wouldn't leave him."

"Of course not. He will remain with you."

Lily gaped at him. Was he in his right mind? After everything they'd been through, everything he'd done to bind her to him and get Danny? "You aren't making sense, Nico."

"No? It is simple enough, *tesoro mio.* We will share our son, as many divorced couples do. He is still my heir, and he will need to spend more time in Montebianco as he grows up. But you will have a house here and will be with him."

Goose bumps prickled her skin. She was so cold all of a sudden. "You're divorcing me, but you want me to remain in Montebianco?"

"I am settling one hundred million of your American dollars on you, *cara,* and more in the future should you need it. You may buy a house on every continent should you wish. But I require you to spend time in Montebianco with our son so that he may learn his heritage and his position. Should he choose not to follow me when he is old enough to do so, that is his right."

Lily stared at the pen in front of her through a blur. He was offering her everything she could have hoped for. Danny would be safe and well. He would only have a part-time father—but that was better than no father. Or, at least it was when that father was Nico. He would not neglect his son, not ever. They could work it out, and her baby would never be in danger again.

Signing was the right thing to do. Earlier, she'd wanted to tell him she would not be a passive participant any longer. They could be married—because she truly hadn't thought he would divorce her—but she would not share his bed and wonder when he would cast her aside. She felt too much when they were together, and she wouldn't torture herself like that.

She deserved a man who loved her the way she did him. She wanted that man to be Nico, but clearly he never would be.

"If you are pregnant, *cara*—"

"I'm not," she said fiercely, not caring when a tear spilled free and dropped onto the paper. She'd gotten that news when she'd woken from her nap. There would be no baby.

"Ah."

She stared at him for a long minute, waiting for what she did not know. Did she expect him to confess his love? To tell her it was an elaborate ruse for some reason she couldn't fathom?

She picked up the pen, hesitated. Would he stop her? But he didn't move.

Lily had to lean closer to see the line. Another tear spilled, landed with a fat plop on his signature. Quickly, she scratched the pen across the line below his, then dropped it and shoved away from the table.

CHAPTER TWELVE

NICO DIDN'T TRULY FEEL the effects of what he'd done until many hours later, when he wandered into the nursery and found it empty. He'd been operating on autopilot, and now...

Now his son was no longer there, no longer ready to smile and babble at him and ask to be picked up. Nico liked holding his boy. The little guy put his arms around his neck and held on tight while Nico carried him around and talked to him in that silly voice parents often used with children. He'd never quite understood the urge to do so until he had his own child.

And then he hadn't cared how ridiculous he might sound, or who might overhear him.

He stood at the crib's edge and gripped the railing tight, staring into the emptiness with an unseeing gaze. Danny was gone, and the knowledge ripped him in two.

How had he managed to let them go? Why had he done it?

Part of him, the part he'd shoved down deep, howled in rage and grief.

He'd done the right thing; he'd given Lily her freedom because she had a right to find happiness with someone she could love. She deserved to be safe and well, to not live in fear. He could give her that much. If it hurt him to do so, he would get over it. She came first.

He could feel the weight of the blue diamond ring he'd given her in his trouser pocket. She'd left it on his pillow before she'd gone, and he'd carried it around for hours now, the solidity of it searing him like a brand. Reminding him of what he'd lost.

A hot, possessive emotion washed over him. He wanted her.

But it wasn't just a sexual need.

She came first. The feeling buffeting him was so strong, so overwhelming, that he wondered how he'd not been bowled over by it sooner.

He'd been happy with Lily and Danny. Lily was the only woman who'd ever seemed to care more about the man than the prince. Hadn't she told him she didn't like the prince? That the man was the one she preferred?

She'd given herself to him when she had no idea who he was, other than plain Nico Cavelli. She hadn't known about the money or the privilege, hadn't known he was from an ancient and royal family. She'd thought he was a foreign student visiting New Orleans for Mardi Gras.

Dio, she *loved* him. Nico couldn't breathe as he gripped the railing. Anguish ripped through him. She'd never said the words, but he knew she did. How had he been so blind? She'd lied to him and he'd believed her.

Madonna diavola, what a fool he was!

She'd told him she didn't love him because she hadn't believed him capable of loving her. Why had he not seen this? Why had he not told her the truth?

Because he *did* love her. She meant everything to him. When Paolo took her, he'd thought he would go mad with the urge to kill the man. Her safety had been his paramount concern. Not his own, not his country's—hers. Hers and Danny's. He would have died for them both if it had been necessary, and to hell with duty.

He was in love with the woman he'd married, the woman

who'd borne his child all alone—and he'd let her go. He'd sent her away because he'd believed she wanted her freedom, that she would be happier without him.

Dio, Dio, Dio.

Nico rubbed his chest, but the raw, empty hole did not go away. He'd let her go because he'd wanted to right the wrong he'd done her when he forced her to marry him.

But, once again, he'd gotten it wrong.

He spun away from the empty crib and strode through the apartment to his office. It was very early in the morning, and he hadn't slept at all, but he had much to do.

This time, he would get it right.

In the end, it was extraordinarily easy to leave her life in Montebianco and return to Port Pierre. She'd kept hoping— through the numbing ordeal of being ferried to the airport, boarding the royal jet and getting settled for the flight—that Nico would suddenly appear and tell her he'd been wrong, that he wanted them both to stay.

But the jet took off and there was no turning back. She'd chosen Port Pierre because it was familiar, but she had no idea where she would truly end up. Perhaps she'd move to Paris, learn French and find a handsome Frenchman to settle down with. The thought was so strange that it seemed like a film she might view rather than an idea about her life. She was wealthy beyond her dreams, yet she felt poorer than ever and sad.

When they landed in New Orleans, Lily took a room in a nice hotel in the French Quarter. She needed to prepare for her return to Port Pierre. She hadn't quite considered the logistics of it when she'd told Nico that's where she wanted to go. He'd ordered the jet made ready without question, and she'd felt that she had to carry through with it or look like a fool.

But if she were truly to return, she would need a place to stay that was big enough to accommodate the full-time nanny and the security team Nico sent with her. She'd thought the bodyguards would return to Montebianco when they delivered her to her destination, but no, they were as permanent as a presidential Secret Service detail. Danny was a prince, and the heir to the Montebiancan throne. He required security. She hadn't escaped the danger after all, no matter how far she'd run.

Lily spent four days in the city, putting off the trip to Port Pierre each morning as she contemplated her next move. She went to see her mother in the treatment facility. Nico had spared no expense in getting the best help possible. Donna Morgan looked better than Lily had ever seen her. Her skin wasn't so sallow, and she was actually filling out a bit. And she asked about her grandson, which shocked Lily and made her cry. When Lily left, Donna asked her to send pictures and to stay in touch. It was more interest in her life than her mother had shown in years and it touched her deeply.

On the sixth day, Lily hired a car and made the hour trek to her hometown. Port Pierre was exactly as she'd left it—and yet everything had changed. She knew she couldn't work at the paper anymore, not when she *was* the news. Everyone stared at her as she made the rounds of the shops and businesses she'd once frequented.

She even went to visit Carla, but it was awkward. Her friend had bought the historic home in Port Pierre's center that she'd always wanted and was fixing it up with the money Nico had paid her. Carla apologized over and over, though Lily told her she understood. But she left the encounter feeling more alone than she ever had. Something had changed between them in the short time Lily was gone, and she knew their relationship would never be the same. They would remain friends, but they would never have that easy camaraderie they'd once had. Their paths had diverged forever.

Lily returned to New Orleans more confused and upset than ever. It really was true that you could never go home again. She was untethered, blowing in the wind like a dried husk, uncertain where she would land or if she would survive the trip. Violent storms were an unfortunate part of life in Louisiana, but you could rebuild after a storm. How did you fix the damage left in your soul when it was a man who'd caused the devastation?

But of course she would survive, she thought angrily. It would just take time.

As if on cue, an afternoon thunderstorm blew into the city, lashing furiously at the windows and cracking booms that frightened Danny and made Signora Cosimo's eyes widen in alarm each time. When it was over, and everyone was soothed, Lily decided to walk the rain-washed streets alone. She needed to release some of her energy, needed to make a decision about what to do next, and she was determined to accomplish it this afternoon.

New Orleans was still a vibrant city, full of equal parts danger and exhilaration. She avoided the decadence of Bourbon Street, instead choosing the more elegant Royal Street a block over. To think she could now walk into any of the fancy shops and buy anything she wanted was still beyond her grasp. She was so accustomed to living frugally, with the exception of her two weeks as the Crown Princess of Montebianco.

Eventually, she had to pass St. Louis Cathedral. She hesitated only a moment before looping around to the front of the building on Chartres Street. The white facade of the church practically glowed in the pale light that remained after the storm had passed. Lily crossed the street to Jackson Square, then turned and looked up at the three spires of the church.

She sighed, then decided to start toward the hotel again. A man ambled toward her through the square and she stopped, struck by how he reminded her of Nico at this distance. He even wore a hooded running jacket, the same as Nico had that first time she'd met him. At the man's back was the Mississippi River, turning golden as a ray of setting sunshine spilled over its surface. A barge glided by in the distance and she focused on it wistfully.

But when her gaze returned to the man, her heart quickened. It could not be…

It took a very long moment for her to realize that her heart had recognized what her eyes still did not want to admit.

"Liliana," he said, drawing up in front of her. His hands were in his jeans pockets, but he took them out and pushed back the hood.

"What are you doing here?" she asked, dumbstruck. It was too much, the sight of him. All her memories of meeting him here two years ago crashed down on her. And everything since. She felt as though she needed to sit, so she retreated to a park bench a few feet away and thunked down on it.

Nico followed, though he stood over her and didn't join her on the bench. He looked…sheepish. And as if he hadn't slept in days. Lines of strain bracketed his mouth, and dark circles lay heavy under his eyes.

His beautiful eyes.

"I want you to marry me," he said.

If he'd announced he was joining the circus, she couldn't have been more surprised. "But you just divorced me. Why would I want to go through it again?"

"Because you love me."

Lily shot up off the bench, heart pounding. "How dare you come here and try to manipulate me this way! What happened,

Nico, did you decide you'd made a mistake and now you want us back?"

"Yes." Said without hesitation.

The steam faded from Lily's tirade. She had not the strength to battle him, not anymore. "You pushed us away. You told us to go."

"I have regretted it every moment since. I made a mistake."

Lily shook her head, tears blurring her eyes. "I can't do this, Nico. I can't go through the ups and downs of a life with you."

"The ups and downs can be quite pleasant, yes?"

"I can't do this," she repeated.

His smile faded. He looked grave, as serious as she'd ever seen him. "I want you, Lily. I want Danny. Come back to Montebianco with me. I will protect you both with my life."

She choked down a sob.

"I can't." She clenched her fists together, fought the urge to scream at the top of her lungs. Her entire body trembled with the opposing forces beating at her. "Oh God, it's not fair! I can't stand a life without you, but how can I manage one with you?"

She whirled around, intent on getting away, but he caught her against him before she'd taken the first step, pressed her cheek to his chest while she clutched his jacket. She wanted to push him away, and yet she couldn't. How pitiful was she?

All she could do was cling to his warmth, his strength. He smelled like home to her, like everything she'd ever wanted in her life. She closed her eyes, drank in his scent.

Beneath her cheek, his heart beat nearly as fast as her own. He pushed her a step back suddenly, tilted her head up with his palms on either side of her face. His eyes were as haunted as she felt as he looked down at her.

"I love you, Lily. Do you hear me? I love you."

She felt the tears slip down her cheeks now, faster than

before. "You don't mean it," she said. "You can't love me. You're supposed to love someone like Antonella—"

"*Never.* I love *you.* No other woman compares to you. You are bright and beautiful, and you love me—"

"I didn't say that!"

His smile was tender. "You didn't have to." He grasped her hand, pressed it to his heart. "Do you feel what you do to me? You see the real me, Lily. You are the only one who ever has, the one who owns me body and soul. If you tell me no now, I will respect that. But I will die inside for every day you are not with me—"

"Stop, Nico," she whispered. "I can't take anymore—"

"It is the truth, *tesoro mio.* I adore you, I adore our baby, I want my life to be full again. It will only be so with you in it."

She stared up at him, her heart careening into territory she didn't understand. But her mind was more cautious. "I want it, too, Nico—but how can I be sure you won't change your mind? That you won't tire of a wife and children? I won't accept girlfriends or royal mistresses or whatever you want to call them."

"Lily, for God's sake, didn't you hear me? I love *you.* Only you. I want no one else. I cannot imagine being with anyone else." He took her by the shoulders, looked her square in the eye. "You told me that you never wanted anyone but me. How can you imagine that I don't know my own heart like you know yours?"

"That's fair," she whispered, her throat aching.

"Tell me you love me, Lily. Tell me you will marry me."

But she couldn't do it just yet. "It's been six days, Nico."

"I was on my way within hours after you left, but my father had a mild heart attack—"

"Oh no! I'm sorry."

"He is well, *cara.* It was very mild, and the drugs dissolved the clot instantly. But I had to return and remain as regent while he was on bed rest."

"Duty called," she said.

"It will often do so. I cannot lie to you about that. Sometimes, I will have to obey the dictates of duty. But I will never do so when your happiness is at stake. Never, *Mi Principessa*."

She toyed with one of the strings on his jacket. "I understand, Nico. And it's one of the things I admire most about you. Your dedication to doing what is right, I mean."

"It has taken me a very long while to get this right." He dropped to one knee, and her breath caught. "Marry me, Liliana. Have babies with me. Make me smile, make me crazy, but most of all, say yes and make me happy."

She blinked down at him. He meant it—oh God, he *meant* it.

"Shouldn't you have a ring?" she teased, joy beginning to bubble inside her soul.

He grinned, fishing something from his pocket. "I do. It is most gaudy and ostentatious, but I have learned my lesson, I assure you. This," he said, slipping the correctly sized blue diamond onto her shaking ring finger, "is merely temporary. Until we can go to the jeweler's and pick out a proper ring together."

Lily clutched the diamond to her. "No, this one is perfect. It's the one you gave me when I said yes to your proposal. I couldn't dream of trading it."

"So you agree to marry me?"

She wrapped her arms around his neck. "I do," she said, then bent to kiss him.

When she finally stopped, he stood and swept her into his arms, twirling her around until she giggled.

Then he set her down and pulled her in close, his hands on her hips. She couldn't mistake that he wanted her when their bodies came into contact.

"I am crazy for you, Lily. *Crazy*." He kissed her thoroughly, groaning when she pressed in against him. But her body ached, too. If she could get him back to the hotel, send Signora Cosimo and Danny down to dinner…

"I have a room," he murmured. "Do you want to come back to it?"

"I would love to."

They hurried through the streets until he pulled up short in front of a building that housed an inexpensive hotel. Lily gaped at him. "It's the same place."

He grinned. "The same room, too."

And then they were inside, tearing at each other's clothes, mouths and bodies desperate to connect again. They never made it to the bed. Nico backed her into the wall and lifted her, then thrust inside her while she wrapped her legs around his waist. Their lovemaking was urgent, intense, and she quickly spiraled to the heights of pleasure, then splintered apart while he relentlessly drove her over the edge.

When it was finished, they slid down the wall to the floor, breathing hard. Lily let her gaze slide over the room. The rose wallpaper was about forty years out-of-date, the furnishings were neat and clean, though slightly scarred and threadbare, and the floor creaked.

"I'm surprised you remembered which room," she said.

He looked indignant. "This place is very special, *cara*. The future king of Montebianco was conceived here."

"And maybe, if we're lucky, a brother or sister."

Nico kissed her and grinned. "I will do my part, Lily. As many times as you deem necessary."

"I'm sure one night won't be enough. We will need to keep trying again and again…."

His smile widened. "And again and again."

"Now you've got the idea." *Men.* Thank God.

Nico laughed. "Until I die of exhaustion, *Mi Principessa,* I live to serve you in all ways."

Lily traced her finger along his beautiful, lush mouth. How had she ever gotten so lucky? *This* was right, so right.

"I love you, Nico Cavelli. Even if you are a prince."

EPILOGUE

THEY WERE MARRIED AGAIN in Montebianco, a big state wedding with television crews and world media coverage. Princess Antonella caught the bouquet, and Donna Morgan looked very elegant and respectable as the mother of the bride. She wasn't finished with her rehabilitation, but she was making progress every day. Lily actually enjoyed spending time with her, and Donna seemed to take the pageantry and protocol of having a royal daughter in stride.

Lily had even managed to recruit the local reporters into her way of thinking. The coverage wasn't always glorious, and falsehoods most definitely made it into the European tabloids, but Lily established a public relations office where she interacted with media representatives for a few minutes each week. She'd quickly become their darling, and she was determined to maintain as much control over her image, and her family's, as possible. She enjoyed meeting with reporters now, and she always felt satisfaction at a job well-done. Public relations, it seemed, was her true calling.

When Nico asked where Lily wanted to honeymoon, she answered without hesitation: the house on the coast. The days were spent making love, playing on the beach with Danny and simply enjoying each other's company. They even returned to the cave, this time with a picnic and a nice blanket, and finished what they'd started the last time.

Lily emerged from the shower after a particularly delightful afternoon in bed with her husband to find him sitting on the floor with their son. He often went and got Danny and brought him into their room while Lily dressed.

Danny stood across from Nico, his little face very serious as he held out his blue dinosaur and said something. Nico's brows drew together, but he smiled and said something back.

Danny shook his head and said it again.

Nico looked up when she walked in. "Help."

"I don't know, Nico."

Danny swung his gaze to Lily, but turned back to Nico. Then he toddled over and threw his arms around Nico's neck. "Baba," he said. "Baba."

And then he set his dinosaur in Nico's lap and walked away.

Nico's eyes were shining as he looked at her. "Did he just say…?"

Lily pressed her hand to her mouth. "Yes."

"Don't cry, Lily," he said, getting up to come and hold her close.

"Same to you."

"Princes don't cry," he said very seriously, even though his eyes were suspiciously wet.

"Of course not," Lily agreed, squeezing him tight.

Then he tilted her head back and kissed her. And in spite of the fact they'd just made love, she wanted him again with a fierceness that always took her breath away.

"You are my happiness," he said, pressing his lips to her forehead. "My soul. Both of you."

"Three of us," she corrected.

He searched her face. "This is true? You are pregnant?"

"I think so, but I will need to be tested."

"Get in bed," he ordered.

"Nico, we just got out of bed."

"No, *you* get in bed. Immediately. I will bring you dinner and—"

She put her hand over his mouth. "We're not living in the Middle Ages. I think I can safely walk around the house, perhaps even swim a bit. Who knows, maybe I can even make love…."

"Very well," he said with a long-suffering sigh. "But no more motorcycle riding."

Lily laughed. "I'm sure I can agree to *that*."

* * * * *

"YOU HAVE MADE him proud," he told her, nodding at her father, feeling benevolent. "You are the jewel of his kingdom."

Finally, she turned her head and met his gaze, her sea-colored eyes were clear and grave as she regarded him.

"Some jewels are prized for their sentimental value," she said, her musical voice pitched low, but not low enough to hide the faint tremor in it. "And others for their monetary value."

"You are invaluable," he told her, assuming that would be the end of it. Didn't women love such compliments? He'd never bothered to give them before. But Gabrielle shrugged, her mouth tightening.

"Who is to say what my father values?" she asked, her light tone unconvincing. "I would be the last to know."

"But I know," he said.

"Yes." Again, that grave, sea-green gaze. "I am invaluable, a jewel without price." She looked away. "And yet, somehow, contracts were drawn up, a price agreed upon and here we are."

There was the taint of bitterness to her words then. Luc frowned. He should not have indulged her—he regretted the impulse. This was what happened when emotions were given reign.

"Tell me, princess," he said, leaning close, enjoying the way her eyes widened, though she did not back away from him. He liked her show of courage, but he wanted to make his point perfectly clear. "What was your expectation? Do not speak to me of contracts and prices in this way, as if you are the victim of some subterfuge," he ordered her, harshly. "You insult us both."

Her gaze flew to his, and he read the crackling temper there. It intrigued him as much as it annoyed him—but either way he could not allow it. There could be no rebellion, no bitterness, no intrigue in this marriage. There could only be his will and her surrender.

He remembered where they were only because the band chose that moment to begin playing. He sat back in his chair, away from her. *She is not merely a business acquisition,* he told himself, once more grappling with the urge to protect her—safeguard her. *She is not a hotel, or a company.*

She was his wife. He could allow her more leeway than he would allow the other things he controlled. At least today.

"No more of this," he said, rising to his feet. She looked at him warily. He extended his hand to her and smiled. He could be charming if he chose. "I believe it is time for me to dance with my wife."

Indulge yourself with this passionate love story that starts out as a royal marriage of convenience, and look out for more dramatic books from Caitlin Crews and Harlequin Presents in 2010!

Sold, bought, bargained for or bartered

He'll take his...

Bride on Approval

Whether there's a debt to be paid,
a will to be obeyed or a business
to be saved...she has no choice
but to say, "I do"!

PURE PRINCESS,
BARTERED BRIDE

by *Caitlin Crews*

#2894

Available February 2010!

HARLEQUIN *Presents*

PREGNANT BRIDES

*Inexperienced and expecting,
they're forced to marry!*

Bestselling Harlequin Presents author

Lynne Graham

brings you the second story
in this exciting new trilogy:

RUTHLESS MAGNATE,
CONVENIENT WIFE
#2892
Available February 2010

Also look for

GREEK TYCOON,
INEXPERIENCED MISTRESS
#2900
Available March 2010

www.eHarlequin.com

HP12892

HARLEQUIN *Presents* EXTRA

**Presents Extra brings you
two new exciting collections!**

LATIN LOVERS

They speak the language of passion!

The Venadicci Marriage Vengeance #89
by MELANIE MILBURNE

The Multi-Millionaire's Virgin Mistress #90
by CATHY WILLIAMS

GREEK HUSBANDS

Saying "I do" is just the beginning!

The Greek Tycoon's Reluctant Bride #91
by KATE HEWITT

Proud Greek, Ruthless Revenge #92
by CHANTELLE SHAW

Available February 2010

REQUEST YOUR FREE BOOKS!

2 FREE NOVELS PLUS 2
FREE GIFTS!

YES! Please send me 2 FREE Harlequin Presents® novels and my 2 FREE gifts (gifts are worth about $10). After receiving them, if I don't wish to receive any more books, I can return the shipping statement marked "cancel". If I don't cancel, I will receive 6 brand-new novels every month and be billed just $4.05 per book in the U.S. or $4.74 per book in Canada. That's a savings of close to 15% off the cover price! It's quite a bargain! Shipping and handling is just 50¢ per book*. I understand that accepting the 2 free books and gifts places me under no obligation to buy anything. I can always return a shipment and cancel at any time. Even if I never buy another book, the two free books and gifts are mine to keep forever.

106 HDN EYRQ 306 HDN EYR2

Name	(PLEASE PRINT)	
Address		Apt. #
City	State/Prov.	Zip/Postal Code

Signature (if under 18, a parent or guardian must sign)

Mail to the **Harlequin Reader Service**:
IN U.S.A.: P.O. Box 1867, Buffalo, NY 14240-1867
IN CANADA: P.O. Box 609, Fort Erie, Ontario L2A 5X3

Not valid to current subscribers of Harlequin Presents books.

Are you a current subscriber of Harlequin Presents books and want to receive the larger-print edition? Call 1-800-873-8635 today!

* Terms and prices subject to change without notice. Prices do not include applicable taxes. Sales tax applicable in N.Y. Canadian residents will be charged applicable provincial taxes and GST. Offer not valid in Quebec. This offer is limited to one order per household. All orders subject to approval. Credit or debit balances in a customer's account(s) may be offset by any other outstanding balance owed by or to the customer. Please allow 4 to 6 weeks for delivery. Offer available while quantities last.

Your Privacy: Harlequin Books is committed to protecting your privacy. Our Privacy Policy is available online at www.eHarlequin.com or upon request from the Reader Service. From time to time we make our lists of customers available to reputable third parties who may have a product or service of interest to you. If you would prefer we not share your name and address, please check here. ☐

HARLEQUIN
Ambassadors

Want to share your passion for reading Harlequin® Books?

Become a Harlequin Ambassador!

Harlequin Ambassadors are a group of passionate and well-connected readers who are willing to share their joy of reading Harlequin® books with family and friends.

You'll be sent all the tools you need to spark great conversation, including free books!

All we ask is that you share the romance with your friends and family!

You'll also be invited to have a say in new book ideas and exchange opinions with women just like you!

To see if you qualify* to be a Harlequin Ambassador, please visit www.HarlequinAmbassadors.com.

Thank you for your participation.

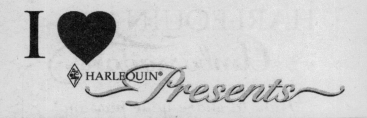